THE REVENANT
AND
THE TOMB

BY

HERMAN P. HUNTER

Credits

Cover Design:

EBook Launch (www.ebooklaunch.com)

Beta Readers:

The Wonderful Mrs. Herman Hunter. Mary Webster.

Editing / Proofreading:

Krista Wagner.

Formatting:
EBook Launch (www.ebooklaunch.com)

I'd like to dedicate this work to the owners and staff of Churchill's in West Bloomfield, who have watched me pound out at least four books over the last few years, down there at the end of the bar. Some of those books I told you about. Some of them I didn't.

But, yeah, one of them finally got published.

CHAPTER 1

"Dangerous deed, laying down gold in a place such as this," Drahm said as he set his flagon back on the tavern table. Halfway through draining the beer from his mug, a single Talen bounced and banged on the worn wood of the rude table; it was a long bar of gold as thick and as long as a man's index finger. A precious thing, it shimmered in the light of a single tallow candle. Finally coming to rest on the worn and stained wood of the table, it lay exposed to the ready glare of greedy eyes.

Drahm's cautious stare briefly fixed on the golden token and then quickly scanned the room. Extending his hand, he reached out and covered his prize before scooping it under his palm.

"Perhaps you should check if it is truly gold," said Halsedric, his keen gray eyes fixed on the older man.

The pair couldn't be more unlike, youth contrasted with wizened age. Halsedric stood tall and proud, a knapsack slung over one shoulder, tight flaxen curls cut trim atop a fair face barely touched by age. His clothes were still stained from the road, and the filth he wore was a testament as to how far he had come to meet the elder guide. Mud stained his trousers and the white sleeves of his shirt and spattered his well-worn leather vest that had seen more than its fair share of the world.

"Later. Sit," Drahm said, sitting up and pointing to a

nearby chair with his clenched fist. A hard man with a hard face, his features were weathered by the elements and long years of hard living. Running from the left edge of his brow, a scar wound down and around his cheek, following the line of his jaw. The bulge of the scar parted the hairs of his beard, which came neatly to a point below his chin. Wool and leather made up most of his garb, durable but weather-worn, hiding a shoddy linen shirt beneath. A long dark gray mane was pulled back and woven into a long braid that ran down the length of his back.

Halsedric unloaded his burden as Drahm quickly slid his prize into an inner pocket of his woolen vest. All the while, he eyed the patrons who stewed and simmered in the darkened expanse of the room. This was indeed a rough place, smoke-filled, greasy, and dim. The low rumble of quiet conversations could be heard in the shadows. With a low dying fire in a distant hearth, the light from cheap candles in their rude holders wasn't enough to give the place life. Perhaps that was by design.

For Halsedric, the smell was enough for him. Stale beer, soured wine, hints of urine, vomit, and worse lingered like a wretched miasma around him. The greasy smoke of the burning tallow stained the rafters. This was an old place where many generations of men came and schemed terrible schemes, given anonymity by the eternal dusk that lived within the walls.

This certainly wasn't the first tavern Halsedric visited, for he had seen many such places in his time. Large timber-framed structures whose walls were made of tree trunks. Logs that were stripped and notched, the gaps on the seams packed with moss and clay. Yet of all the seedy establishments he found himself in, this place held a distinct rank as one of the most blighted.

Taking up his flagon again, Drahm leaned back in his chair, the wood creaking in reply. He held it in the air for a moment before taking a swift drink and cradling the wooden mug in his hands. "Aye. You got my attention." His voice ground in his throat, hinting of his advanced age and habitual use of a pipe. "I suspect I already know what you are goin' to ask 'o me."

"I need a guide," answered Halsedric.

"Aye. I know these parts well. Might I ask where you are a-goin'?"

Settling into what little comfort his chair provided, Halsedric continued his keen-eyed stare. "They say you know the lands of the Horn of Torgiv well."

Coy, Drahm stared into the remaining beer of his flagon. The candle light flickered a bit, casting shadows on the lines of his face. "Aye," he said with a subtle nod.

"I need someone who can lead us to the southern slope."

Drahm let loose a discontented sigh. The interest that his face once showed diminished.

"Is there a problem?" said Halsedric. There was a bland quality to his expression, like that of an innocent boy, unaware of the world and its dangers. Yet, there was also confidence that shone through. The confidence of a man who had known peril and was unafraid.

"Have you any idea what lingers there, friend?" Quick and cynical, Drahm's glance—though brief—spoke volumes. This was not the first time someone had asked for such a service, much to their eventual regret.

"I am aware of the peril."

"Are you? Tell me, son, what know you 'o them

lands?"

With a slight grin, Halsedric replied, "I know that you are one of the few who dare venture there. All of the others I asked politely declined."

"Aye."

"So, you will accept?"

Lazily placing his mug back on the table, Drahm answered, "See here, friend. If'n you pay up front, I'll take you as far as I deem wise. I may be old. I ain't no fool."

Leaning forward, and setting his arm on the table, he lowered his voice and spoke with a frankness that was both bold and dismissive. "Them lands ain't for the faint 'o heart. Yerch up there, an' worse."

"Yerch do not concern me."

"They should," Drahm answered with a hard stare. "But they ain't th' only peril you'll face."

"That is none of your concern."

Lifting up slightly, Drahm rubbed his face with his hand, part in frustration, and part in disgust. "You ain't th' first, you know."

"You will be well paid."

"Pay got nothin' to do with it. Aye, I've made good coin off them fools comin' here an' askin' the same as you."

"And you refused them?"

"A man has to make a livin'."

Halsedric's gaze hardened. "And yet, knowing what you know, you took them. Does that not trouble you?"

Drahm lifted up slightly. "I sleeps well, if'n that's what you mean."

"How then?"

Incredulous, Drahm's irritation at Halsedric's

persistent questioning started to show on his face. His eyes looked away and with a disgruntled sigh, he spoke. "Cuz each of them I says the same. But I says the same as I says to you."

"Which is?"

"That gold is gold, an' bein' a tracker is my trade. I do it well. Many I've took to the land of the Aranach. An' of them, bloody and rent they returned. If'n they return at all."

Eyes shifting away for a moment, Halsedric considered the warning of the guide. "Fair enough. Your concern is noted."

"Son, heed my words," Drahm said, his words pleading, though his tone and expression were far from it. "They all go, bold an' boastin'. Sedric Strongarm, Thenos th' Mighty Blade. Some for glory, most for riches. What they find is ruin an' death. Every one. No exception. An' you will be no diff'nt."

"Your warnings are well heeded," Halsedric said, his former composure returning to his face. "I assure you, we seek neither glory nor riches."

His eyes turned downward for a moment, before looking up once more. "Have you seen it?"

Brows furrowed, Drahm asked sharply, "Seen what?"

"The entrance."

Slowly, Drahm sat up, a sort of stunned confusion washing over him. "You know of it?"

With a slow, silent nod, Halsedric answered.

Drahm had to think for a moment before answering. In the distance, the legs of a bench scraped against the wooden floor, accompanied by soft footfalls that disappeared in the distance. This got the old guide's attention and his eyes sought the darkened forms that lay beyond Halsedric.

"Aye," Drahm answered, haltingly. "Once. When I dared venture close."

"And what lay within?"

Shaking his head in reply, Drahm answered, "Don't know. Don't care."

"Those that did venture in, what did they speak of?"

"Ghosts, some said. Others spoke of demons. One claimed a fell voice in th' dark. All of `em half-mad."

"When can we depart?"

The sudden change in conversation broke the grim spell that lay on the aged guide. He looked confused for a moment, and then his head turned to his beer. Taking up his flagon, he reclined in his chair once more and stretched out his legs. He pondered the question for a moment, cradling his flagon in both hands. "Two days to gather provisions, an' then we can be off. I'll need payment ere we depart."

"How much?"

"How many are you?"

"Make plans for four, though there are only three of us," said Halsedric. "We have made camp just north of the village. Find us there on the `morrow, and you will be paid."

"Twelve silver Anders for supplies. Ten gold Anders for th' journey. Half now. Half when we make final camp."

"A fair price," Halsedric said as he stuck out his hand.

Drahm looked at the gesture for a moment and

paused, obviously pondering the wisdom of the agreement. With reluctance, he set his flagon on the table once more, leaned forward in his chair, and grasped Halsedric's hand, the sure gesture of a pact that had been sealed. Drahm offered a queer look when he felt the soft, supple flesh of his client's hands.

"These are not th' hands `o an adventurer."

"Oh?"

Releasing his grip, Drahm took up his flagon again and leaned back in his chair. "Your hands feel like those of a kept maiden or a silk-swaddled nobleman's son."

Cocking an eyebrow, Halsedric let his hand fall. "Oh?"

Drahm shrugged as he took a quick sip of his beer. "Well, we'll know your measure in due time."

"How so?"

"Did I not say droppin' gold in a place like this was an ill thought?"

With a knowing smile, Halsedric closed his eyes and returned a slow nod. "Ah. You refer to the five men seated behind us? Yes. I saw them as I entered."

"Did you, now?"

"There are three sitting there now, yes?"

Leaning his head to one side, Drahm squinted as his eyes probed the dim light and haze beyond them. "Aye."

"That means two are awaiting me outside, with two to follow, and a third as a runner should I decide to slip out the back."

His brows lifting in surprise, Drahm answered with a single "Aye."

"I assure you, they will not be a problem. I am not so much a fool as to enter this place with a full purse."

"As you say, son."

"And one other thing," Halsedric said as his grin faded and his keen, terrible eyes returned, "I am not your son."

"You look mighty young—"

Reaching down and picking up his pack, Halsedric interrupted, "Of one thing I can assure you, appearances can be quite deceiving."

"We shall see, aye?"

Legs scraped against the filthy wooden floor as Halsedric stood from his chair, the back of his knees pushing the seat away. Slinging the strap of his pack over his shoulder, he said softly, "Yes, we shall."

With a shallow bow, he added, "Good evening to you, sir. See you on the 'morrow."

Lifting his mug in reply, a disbelieving smile graced the face of the guide beneath the twisted and uneven hair that sprung from his face.

Turning sharply, Halsedric disappeared into the drear of the tavern, weaving his way through the benches, tables, and chairs that seemed to haphazardly clutter the space.

Making his way straight to the main door, he stopped as he passed the trio. They were sitting on benches that flanked a long table. Two on one side and one on the opposing bench, they were a rough and motley crew.

He faced the men as a hush suddenly fell over the dimly lit room. Lean faces, unshaven, with dark long hair and hungry eyes stared back at him. The expressions they held belied clear surprise by Halsedric's actions.

Halsedric smiled and bowed slow and shallow. "Gentlemen," he said in a stately voice, leaving the trio confused. Facing the door once more, he continued his trek to the exit.

"Fool," Drahm muttered to himself as he quickly drained the remains of his flagon. With a satisfied grunt, he held the empty wooden mug up high and yelled, "Innkeep? 'Nother beer. Now, curse you!"

CHAPTER 2

Halsedric didn't have to hear the door of the tavern close behind him. Nor did he have to hear the sound of hard leather thumping and scuffing the wooden stairs of the establishment. He already knew that three men followed him out of the tavern; the three he passed as he left. Ahead, two men waited on the road—their accomplices—dark silhouettes against the night, the silvery beams from the waxing moon betraying them in the black.

Amber light from the dirty windows of the tavern streamed out onto the road, painting Halsedric in an unwelcome glow. There was no wondering what was going to happen next. Five men in the night, three behind and two ahead. They were going to rob him. They were going to rob him, and leave him for dead. That's how this was all supposed to work. Letting his knapsack slowly slide to the ground, Halsedric turned to face the trio of men as they approached.

Those hungry eyes fixed upon him. One of the three stopped and knelt, pulling a dagger from a high-topped boot, the others pulling blades from their belts. As their pace slowed, their blades stuck out before them, a wordless threat of what resisting might bring.

Halsedric stood tall, his eyes alternating between the faces of the men and the weapons they displayed. His ears heard the slow approach of the others down the road. While his back was to them now, they were never very far from his mind.

"Bad night for strangers to be about," said the man in the center of the three. Halsedric had identified him as their leader back in the tavern—they were always the easiest to spot. He stood taller than the others, with sunken cheeks and a gaze that lingered somewhere between cunning predator and merciless brute.

None of them were particularly imposing, all three being on the slender side. Altogether, they reminded him of the pack dogs of the southern wilds. None of them were imposing on their own, but they were intelligent, and collectively they could be deadly. Creatures that target the weak when they can, and run from the strong when they must. They had the numbers and they assumed that was all they needed.

Leather resting against hard-packed earth, the strap of the sack came free from Halsedric's hands. He looked at the trio of men, then down at their weapons. His head twisted slightly, noting the approach of the others from behind.

"What you have in that pack `o yours?"

Pausing for a moment, Halsedric replied, "Listen well, friend. Return to the tavern and leave me in peace."

His statement caused confusion amongst the three ruffians. Halsedric watched as the trio exchanged befuddled glances with one another.

Behind him was the crunch of stones and dirt made by the sound of approaching feet. The pair at his back slowed and stopped. Ten paces? Twenty? Halsedric wasn't about to turn and look.

"You're not the one here givin' orders. Now I asked, what's in the bag?" The haggard leader of the ragged crew shook his head woefully as he spoke.

"Where's the gold?" said the one to the left. Despite having features that resembled a scarecrow, he had a brawler's voice, both hearty and rough.

"We've seen it. Hand it over," barked the one to the right, holding up the point of his dagger.

Sighing, Halsedric closed his eyes momentarily, his head bowing as if in some sort of silent prayer. The moment passed quickly, and once more, he eyed the leader of the gang.

Halsedric's voice said more than his words. He was unimpressed. "Son, I have faced far worse than you and your kin. I urge you again," he said, lifting his hand and waving it in a lazy circle in the air, "turn about and go back into the tavern. Have an ale or three."

His head tilted to the side, the leader answered, "An' what if we don't, aye?"

A stern look was the reply.

They waited a time, expecting more to his response. When their patience expired, the leader shrugged. "So it is. Rudd, take the pack."

The one to the right took several steps forward, cautious at first. With his blade held forward, his next few steps were anxious shuffles. Head up, dagger out, crouching down lower with each pace as Rudd's left hand reached out for the pack. His eyes were fixed on those of Halsedric as his hand inched closer to the crumpled leather satchel on the ground.

In the blink of an eye, Halsedric reached down and grabbed the wrist of Rudd that held the dagger. With a singular motion, Halsedric twisted the wrist around with such force that the dagger fell from Rudd's grip.

With a yelp, the attacker fell to one knee. Halsedric's grip was like an iron vice. A rending pain went up and down Rudd's arm, followed by a cold jolt. The man winced, struggled, tried to wrench free as he lifted himself vainly to a slight crouch.

Pulling the man forward, Halsedric let his right fist fly, connecting with the bridge of his assailant's nose. A sharp crack followed as his knuckles smote hard the thin bones of Rudd's face. What followed was a weak grunt as the man lost his footing and fell backwards, sliding across the dirt.

While Rudd's free hand reached to protect the shattered remains of his nose, Halsedric held him firmly by the wrist. Despite Rudd pulling and kicking, Halsedric maintained a firm grip on the arm of the man, much in the same way a child might hold a rag doll. Rudd struggled to no avail. The muffled noises he made had a pathetic quality to them, the wordless rumblings of a man who was down for the count.

Lifting his head, Halsedric stared at the leader of this pitiful crew. He wasn't afraid of any of them. After several seconds, Halsedric let Rudd drop, the man hitting the ground with a thump.

A sudden, palpable hesitation came over the attackers, and in the dim light Halsedric could see it. Just cunning enough to hesitate, the leader of the ruffians was not quick to respond. He stood there for a time, silent in the dark, measuring his foe. When he did speak, it was low, resembling the growl of an angry dog.

"Get `em."

The others stood there tense and anxious, indecision and fear keeping them restrained. The leader had to repeat the command a second time, the growl changing to a bark. "Get `em, I said!"

Halsedric's head turned this way and that as three of the group closed in on him, daggers forward. Inching forward wary and uncertain, they were like hunters with spears approaching an angry bear in its den. Men who knew the peril of the task at hand. Men who were fully aware of the damage a cornered bear could do with its claws and teeth. Leather soles scraped dirt, dark forms shuffled closer, then stopped. In unison they lunged, darting forward.

The tip of one dagger thrust itself at Halsedric's abdomen. Halsedric's hand moved as quick as lightning, intercepting the stroke, grabbing the wrist that held the knife. In a flash, fist connected with the attacker's jaw. At once, blood, spit, and teeth spewed in a spray from the ruffian's mouth. The blow landed like a hammer, followed by a grunt and a crunching sound as bone snapped beneath flesh. The attacker crumpled to the ground in a heap.

Halsedric turned to face the two assailants approaching from behind. This time, he wasn't so lucky. The point of a dagger pierced his clothes and flesh, striking just below the collar on his right side. It was a lucky strike to say the least. The attacker stumbled as he moved in, losing his footing in the dirt. As the blade cut deep, a thump reverberated through Halsedric's frame followed by the cold, sharp sensation of pain.

Teeth clenched tightly together and groaning harshly, Halsedric's face twisted with pain. As devastating

14

as the strike was, the blow was not enough to bring him down. Swift and purposeful, his right arm thrust upward, grabbing the man by the arm and pulling him about. With an unnatural strength and fortitude, he sent one man flying into another, knocking both of the approaching attackers to the ground.

From the fallen pair, a cry rose as one man rolled off the other. Sticking up from the abdomen of one of the men was the handle of a dagger, the blade having sunk hilt-deep into flesh and vitals. At once, the man twisted to his side, legs pulled up, hands clasping against the wound.

With the moans and wails of the fallen filling the night, Halsedric pulled free the blade that stuck out from his shoulder. Staring angrily at the weapon in the dark, he used his left hand to feel the wound. It was then that a second knife struck him from behind, somewhere in the back.

The leader of the pack made his move, striking a critical and devastating blow. Wily as a stalking wolf, he had waited until the others had gone while he stood back and watched. It was a cunning move.

Halsedric grunted, his right knee buckling as the leader's blade pulled free. In the shock of the cut, his fingers opened suddenly and the dagger he was holding fell from his grip. By all accounts, Halsedric was a doomed man—stabbed twice, the blood flowing from each wound. But then, unexpectedly, he righted himself, standing straight. As the leader came in for another swift thrust, Halsedric turned and dodged to one side.

The leader of the ruffians overextended his thrust. Off-balance, the man lurched clumsily forward. Halsedric moved in, grabbing him by the left arm with both hands, spinning him about. When Halsedric released his grip, the leader of rogues flew head first into the thick timbers of the tavern wall. A hard thump reverberated through the dense wood. The man landed with such a force, that it no doubt rattled the floorboards. Stunned, the thin man slumped to the ground, visibly defeated.

Dirt and stone shifted and crunched as the only un-injured attacker recovered, scrambling to his feet. For a time, he and Halsedric locked eyes. The bold predator's eyes now looked like that of a scared rabbit as the would-be thief hesitated, held in fear like a deer in headlights. Instead of renewing his assault, the man turned and ran, stumbling and falling after a few long strides. Rolling around on the hard dirt, he recovered and turned back to face Halsedric one last time. His courage as tattered and threadbare as his clothes, he continued his dash into the night, leaving his fellows to their fate.

For a time, Halsedric looked around at the remains of the battle. Two men rolled around on the ground wounded and wailing, one with a knife in his gut, an-other with a hand over his face. A third lay there groaning, eyes closed, blood trickling out the side of his mouth, the darkness covering the swelling on his face. Their leader grabbed feebly at the timbers of the tavern trying in vain to right himself, only to fall back to the ground like a man stewed in too much wine and ale.

Reaching clumsily around behind him, Halsedric probed the gash in his leather vest. Squirming with dis-comfort, he traced the wound with his fingers. Retracting his hand, he looked down upon his fingers, painted black, the fluid warm and slightly sticky—blood. A lot of blood.

Dumbfounded at first, Halsedric inhaled with a wince, grumbling under his breath and shaking his head. "Fool. Stupid fool. Always mind your back."

The leader of the thieves tried again in vain to pull himself to his feet, only to fail. The sound of it distracted Halsedric and the frown on his lips turned tight and angry. Filled with wrath, he focused it in full on the leader.

Approaching the man with the knife in his gut, Halsedric stared at him for a second. Kneeling and batting away the man's hands, he reached in and grabbed the hilt, pulling the weapon free. Screaming and howling like never before, the wounded ruffian moved his hands, fruitlessly covering the hole in his gut.

With a scowl on his face, Halsedric rose and walked slowly over to the fallen leader. Lording over the man, he stood there for a moment as the man looked back, dazed.

Once hungry and vile, the eyes of the leader were now pained and confused. Pathetic, in a way, his cunning and bravado had departed him. Despite his anger, a brief wave of pity washed through Halsedric. The man's clothes were rough and poor, no doubt due to the hardscrabble hard life he led. Still, this was no excuse for robbing a man, nor killing him. The wave was brief, however, serving only to temper the justice the warrior was to deliver.

Kneeling down, Halsedric's pale eyes stared hot at the man who sought to take his life. There was little the ruffian could do other than shake his head and plead. Whatever words he tried to say, they came out in a babble as Halsedric listened, dispassionate, unimpressed.

Grabbing the man's wrist, Halsedric lifted it up, placing it steady against the crest of a timber. Using the full force of his anger, he plunged the dagger through the flesh of the palm, pinning the hand to the wall of the tavern, the blade digging greedily into the fibers of the wood.

A horrible scream rose from the pinned man in response. Stunned and in a fog, the pain of his rent flesh cut through everything, the man's senses returning to him in an instant.

Grabbing the man by the hair, Halsedric pulled back his head and leaned in. "Come take the gold now, dog."

Halsedric let loose the man's mane. Grunting from the pain he felt, Halsedric stood and shuffled over to where his knapsack lay. Hesitant, he bent down, stopping slightly as a shock of pain ran up his spine and down his leg. Undaunted, he took up the pack, grimacing as he threw it over his right shoulder. Stepping over the legs and limbs of his beaten opponents, he walked away with a slight limp, disappearing into the night.

In such a place as this, no one came out of their shelters, questioning the ruckus in the street. It was safer that way.

CHAPTER 3

Morning had broken. Cakes were cooking on hot stones warmed by the campfire as Halsedric grabbed his sword. A rustling from far off was heard. The events of the night before made him wary of potential reprisals from friends or relatives of the men he left lying on that dirt track of a road. Despite the skill and the prowess of his two other companions at battle, a fight was the last thing he wanted right now.

What approached had a cadence that was slow, four-legged, and heavy. Their horses grumbled and milled around the campsite unrestrained or corralled, seemingly unconcerned. One of the horses snorted softly. Halsedric replied to the silvery-white beast, "Yes, I hear it too."

They were a strange breed, the horses, gifted to them by the Lord of Elenur for their use. Lenogala they were so named by the Elanni. Intelligent in their own right, swift as the wind and tireless, they were apt beasts for Halsedric and his mission. He had grown used to their company, though it took several years to learn how to converse with them. More than merely beasts of burden, they had uses far beyond travel.

Tulvgir knelt by the fire, warming himself with the heat of the coals. His mace lay at his right, well within reach. Hungrily, he eyed several cakes as they cooked on a hot stone. Hearing the commotion of the others, he made a discontented sound like the grumble of a bear. "What now?"

Looking past the horses into the thin forest that surrounded him, Halsedric was quiet, his eyes barely blinking and his ears straining. The coals of the fire popped and wisps of smoke confounded his sense of smell. Yet, the one thing his ears ached to hear above all was the signal—the call of the Yellow Jay.

It was a second or two before he heard it. A twitter, and then a long whistle. Just one, then silence.

"A lone rider," Halsedric said in half a whisper.

Tulvgir grumbled louder and his ruddy face made a hard frown beneath the thick whiskers that covered his mouth, jaws, and chin. Slowly, he reached down and wrapped his meaty fingers around the handle of his weapon before rising to his feet. "I hunger. And if there is one thing I detest, it is burnt cakes."

While Halsedric stood a whole head taller than Tulvgir, his companion was by no means the lesser of the two. Wodemen—as men called them—were renowned for many things, strength and endurance being first and foremost. The attributes were mostly a consequence of the blood that flowed through their veins, though no less a factor were the hills and mountains in which they lived. Surefooted and proud, Tulvgir was muscular and tough, with an appetite to match. It was said that one Wodeman could eat as much as three or four men—a fabrication of sorts, though not without merit. They were fond of beer, that was undisputed. So fond of ale, it was said that their young suckled at a cask. Tall tales, of course.

"I hate a fight on an empty stomach," Tulvgir remarked as he lifted his mace up high. His hair was like the color of the coals of the fire and as thick as moss. Two braids hung down from his temples, each bounded by silver clasps studded with amethyst, a third, longer braid trailing down his back. His style of dress gave him the appearance of a miniature ox, being made of tailored cowhide that was brown and streaked with red. Heavy boots covered heavy feet, their familiar thump on hard earth being something of a constant in their travels together.

Bluish steel formed the head of Tulvgir's mace, secured to a solid iron shaft, a weapon that was as heavy as it looked. Eight wedge-shaped prongs arrayed themselves in a circular pattern, creating a striking surface that both battered and cut at the same time. An atypical weapon for one of his kind, it was forged for him by his father and presented to him when he came of age. A weapon whose blows to unprotected flesh could be devastating, if not gruesome to say the least. And a weapon whose strange alloy had seen more than its fair share of conflict.

Halsedric looked down at his traveling companion at his side, waiting for their unseen visitor. "If it bothers you that much, I will make more." The reply was little more than a disbelieving grunt from the Wodeman.

Halsedric squinted, his eyes doing their best to scan every detail from afar. It wasn't long before this task bore fruit. A horse approached from the surrounding wood, its rider old and wary. Moving at a patient pace, the muscular beast had a hide with a buckskin hue and a mane that was as black as a crow's breast. The casual pace was no doubt premeditated, Halsedric assumed, typical of one who knew well how to approach a campsite of strangers. Hood up, the rider dressed in leathers that looked well-worn and mottled.

Halsedric exhaled slowly as he spotted the fringes of a gray mane from beneath the hood. Removing his hand from the hilt of his sword, he said with a note of muted relief, "Our guide."

"Hrumph," Tulvgir answered, letting the head of his mace fall before turning away. "Best to flip those cakes myself."

The soft crunch and rustle of long dead leaves heralded the arrival of Drahm, the pace of his horse slowing even more. One arm raised in greeting, the old man gave a nod as he spoke, "Hail there, young fellow."

"Welcome, friend," Halsedric answered grim-faced, with a nod. "Come to accept the offer, I presume?"

Strangely amused, Drahm shifted in his saddle, a grin and a chuckle saying all Halsedric need know. "Aye. For what you pay, the gold is worth the risk."

For a time, Drahm sat there on his beast, his eyes sizing up the pair. However, when his gaze fell on Halsedric, it lingered, traveling along his shoulder before fixating at a spot on his upper right chest. There in the leather vest, a dark stain was seen along with the last stitches of a hastily mended section, evidence of the previous night's activity.

Hands pressing on the fore of his saddle, he looked to one side and then the other. "No guard? Act `o folly in these parts." The words sounded awkward as his attention shifted quickly, fearful of being too obvious with his stare. With a hard look at Halsedric, he added, "Truer still, given th' reputation `o the village you're near."

His eyes looking past Drahm momentarily, Halsedric stepped away, approaching a pile of branches and splintered wood they had gathered the night before. From them, he took up a flat shake of wood roughly the width of his hand and twice the length. His attention quickly fixed on the path from whence Drahm arrived. Raising up the piece of wood, he waved it in the air and whistled to the seemingly empty forest. Tossing the fragment into the air, a second or two passed as the object went up several feet, spinning as it did. As it fell back to the ground, a different whistle was heard—the deceptively soft sound of a fletched arrow cutting the air. The arrow itself passed above the heads of horse and rider alike before striking the floating target square, knocking it away. The travel of the missile ended soon after, finding a home in the trunk of a nearby tree. The silvery-white horses parted with a flurry of movement and grumbles as the chip bounced along the hard ground, finally coming to rest in a cluster of high weeds.

The spectacle made Drahm instantly sit back in his seat, and his head turned back with a shocked snap. For several moments, he scanned the wilds behind him, his trained eyes seeking movement and finding nothing.

Slowly, the gaze of the wizened guide sought out Halsedric once more. "Filled with surprises an' such, master Nolan."

Returning Drahm's gaze with a confident stare, Halsedric answered, "If I was Nolan once, I have long left that behind. So, you will guide us, yes?"

"About that," Drahm shifted once more, taking up his reins, nervously eying the terrain behind, "seems there was a bit 'o trouble, the night past."

If the display Drahm saw unnerved him, he didn't show it. Halsedric took that as a good sign. The old guide was a man not easily scared away. Drahm's eyes darted to the dark stain on Halsedric's breast before quickly looking away.

Instinctively, Halsedric pulled at his vest near his right shoulder. Head tilting to one side, he answered, "Trouble?"

Looking both ways and lifting himself up in his saddle, Drahm went on. "Them men you greeted in the tavern? Seems someone gave 'em quite a thrashin' not long after you departed. Left one with a broken jaw, an' missin' a few teeth. Don't think the tother be breathin' through his nose anytime soon. An' the one that got pinned to the wall with his own dagger? They had to chisel him free."

"That is disconcerting to hear. Any word on who could have done this terrible deed?"

With that, as he pulled a steaming cake off of the stone, Tulvgir snorted his amusement. Tenderly, he held his meal in his meaty palm. Steam rose from the cake.

"As I hears it, leastwhiles from them's that could talk, ten men fell on 'em in the night, beatin' 'em with rods of iron."

Staring back as the old man spoke, Halsedric lent neither a smile or frown to the account. His eyes had a most disinterested glare.

"'Twas one, however. Said he saw it all. Told this strange tale, he did, of one man doin' the deed. Nothin' but his fists, he said, it bein' dark and all. Said he dropped the first two, just like that. One 'o the brothers got him good in the shoulder ere the stranger took him down."

"Stranger?"

"Aye," Drahm answered with a nod. "Young, he said. Short hair an' tight curls atop his crown. Much like yourself."

"That is quite a coincidence."

"Aye, 'tis true," Drahm answered, his eyes narrowing.

"Well, then, the trouble has at least passed," Halsedric answered as he started to turn away just as Drahm piped up.

"Most of them boys were brothers. One a cousin," Drahm continued, his voice having a certain urgency to it. "A well-known lot here in these parts."

Tiring of the wordplay, Halsedric returned Drahm's serious stare with one of his own. "Speak plainly, if you have any more to say. You come here to deliver a message?"

With that, Drahm threw his head back with a cracked sort of cackle that lasted several moments. From deep in his throat he brought up something thick and wet before spitting it out on the ground below him. His horse snorted and swerved as he answered Halsedric with a grin. "'Taint got no love for that pack 'o curs. Been a bundle 'o trouble, they has, an' for some time now. Thieves an' brigands they are. An' they gots what was comin' to 'em."

His grin faded beneath the scraggly wild whiskers on his face. "But them boys were Jethlo's kin. And Jethlo? He's a heap 'o trouble you ain't known."

"Thank you for the warning, friend—"

"Come the 'morrow, he'll be here with twenty 'o his kin, wantin' vengeance. His sons being mangled and all. No doubt lookin' for you."

"Your warning is noted."

"My price has gone up."

Halsedric stood there and stared for a moment, not quite believing what his ears heard. "Say that again?"

"Jethlo don't scare me much," Drahm said with a slight grin. "But, if you're still needin' a guide, I'll need more for my services. Costs go up when you're in a rush, an' I'll need a few coin to buy silence when folks 'round these parts start askin' questions."

One eye closed, Halsedric pondered this for a moment, wondering after the sincerity of Drahm's offer. "How much?"

"Pay three Talens more, if'n that's all you got. I got coin enough, I think, to cover the cost. Coin or Talens, don't bother me much."

Pulling another sizzling cake from the stone, Tulvgir cradled the round, flat mass as it steamed in his fingers. "Don't do it," he warned before blowing on his meal to cool it. "He will take the money and run."

Drahm looked past Halsedric and made an awful grumble in his throat. "My word is my word," he said in protest. "Ain't broke my word yet, an' I ain't about to break it now."

Tulvgir shook his head as he bit away half of his cake.

Halsedric, however, seemed less suspicious. "Fair enough," he said before turning away. A pile of saddle-bags lay nearby. He approached them, knelt, and started rummaging around.

Drahm watched intently as Halsedric shuffled the contents of two small pouches, his eyes fixed on another dark spot on Halsedric's lower back. A similar dark stain peered out from beneath the leather vest where the blood of the knife wound soaked his shirt.

The attention of the guide shifted away as his ears detected the faint clinking of gold and silver being shifted from one to the other. Before long, one of the pouches was stuffed away, the flap closed on a large leather bag.

Rising to his feet, Halsedric turned, tying the leather strap tight around the pouch he cradled in one hand. He stopped and tossed the precious contents to Drahm. The bag arced and fell into the awaiting palms of the guide, the gold within settling hard with a crunch.

Drahm lifted the pouch feeling the heft of the precious metal within, eying it with a mixture of envy and surprise.

"It should all be there. If not, we will settle your fee when you return," said Halsedric, his anxious eyes fixed on the guide.

Lifting up the leathery pouch once more, Drahm nodded, satisfied. "Much appreciated. Be ready ere I return. I want to be off ere the setting sun, or we ain't leavin' at all."

"We will be ready," assured Halsedric.

As Drahm took the reins of his mount, Halsedric piped up, "What if one of those villagers let slip where we are or where we are going? And this Jethlo decides to pursue?"

Drahm sniffed. "Where we go? Heh. I think no. The man is a brute an' a snake. But even his kind ain't fool enough to follow after us where we a-goin'. Nah. He'll brood and wait for you to come back." With keen eyes, he added, "If'n you come back."

With little else to say, Drahm turned his horse about and departed. As his horse shambled its way back toward the village, Drahm took time to glance about, looking for the spy that evaded his skilled and suspicious eyes. Before long, he and his horse disappeared into the surrounding wilderness as Halsedric watched.

"That coin is gone and gone," Tulvgir said, as he wandered up next to Halsedric. A pale cake was rolled up between his fingers. He took a bite, taking most of the cake with it, brushing the remains from the whiskers on his upper mouth and chin.

"I know his type. He will return," Halsedric assured.

Turning his head slightly toward the Wodeman, he added, "When you are done stuffing that empty belly of yours, break camp and make ready to depart. I want us ready before the sun is high in the sky."

His attention turned to the forest beyond. With a whistle and a wave, he called in their mysterious guard before returning back to the fire.

The horses milled and moved, one snorted while another dug curiously at the forest floor. Halsedric addressed the silvery white beasts amidst a drab wilderness of brown, green, and gray, speaking in a foreign, flowing tongue. As if they understood his speech, the horses took note and nodded.

As Halsedric returned back to the fire, Tulvgir looked down at the crumbling remains of the cake in his hand. Sighing discontentedly, he muttered, "What I would give for a full mug of ale or two."

CHAPTER 4

"You nev'r said a woman was a-comin'," Drahm barked angrily. Furious eyes quickly scanned the maiden before him, his face twisting at the sudden reveal. Bending forward like a reed pressed by the wind, his lined and weathered face stretched as he continued. "Did you not understand where we are a-goin'?"

Halsedric was calm and unfazed by the guide's outrage. "She is more than capable, I assure you."

Drahm had just returned from the village with supplies and an additional pack horse in tow. After getting a good glimpse of Herodiani, he all but leapt from his saddle. His boots thumped nearly as hard as the hooves of his horses as he stormed up to confront the trio as they were breaking camp.

"Capable?" Drahm's face stretched again as his peppered brows lifted high on his forehead. "A sliver o' years less an' she'd be a child."

There was no denying Drahm's claim, for Herodiani was a picture of youth in full bloom. Lithe and small was her frame, and her face was fair and without flaw. Long, golden tresses fell down from her crown, framing her face. Were it not for the travel-worn clothes that garbed her and the moss green cloak that shrouded most of her body, one might imagine her in a formal dress with bright ribbons in her hair. She was truly the image of a woman full in the flower of beauty, a face whose innocent youth was unspoiled by the world and its hard realities.

Only a shade taller than the Wodemen, Herodiani seemed small in contrast to Halsedric. In one hand she grasped the bent frame of a bow that was nearly as large as her. While not physically imposing, she had a stare that, were it a sword, might have rent the guide to shreds. Her eyes were blue, beautiful and hard like crystal, deep set and defiant. Her back stiffened at his words and her mouth narrowed as her lips strained to hold back her true thoughts.

"That child is older than some of the trees that litter these hills," Tulvgir answered with a gruff sort of laugh. He stood proud near the smoldering campfire, hand resting on the handle of his mace as it stuck up, its head resting on the ground.

"She is of the Elanni," Halsedric added.

The bending brows on Drahm's forehead now crashed into a crease as his forehead twitched slightly. "What say you?"

"Elanni." Halsedric said. "The Fair Folk. The Ageless. Surely you have heard of them?"

"Aye." Drahm's head bobbed. "I heard of 'em. I heard lots 'o stories in my time. Don't mean none 'o 'em are true."

"Well, this one is true."

"I care not a wit how old she be," Drahm protested, waving his hand in Herodiani's direction. "Look at 'er. She's naught but a babe. She'd nev'r last in a stand-up fight."

"And yet, she evaded your eyes well enough," Tulvgir piped up, a growing contempt for the old man barely hidden in his voice.

"Oh so that's how she's gonna fight? Hide'n behind a rock somewheres?"

"You saw what she could do with a bow," Halsedric countered.

Pointing to the bow, Drahm replied mockingly, "That thing?" He held his hand out. "Let me inspect this fine magic bow, 'lil girl."

Herodiani was reluctant to give up her weapon, shooting a curious glance at Halsedric.

In reply, Halsedric offered a patient nod, though it was clear from her expression it wasn't the answer she was seeking. Holding out the horn of her weapon, she extended her bow for Drahm's easy reach.

Drahm snatched the weapon, rough and quick. Skeptical, he scanned the features of the weapon. It was an elegant thing, precise and well-crafted. His hand clasped the leather of the grip tightly as his initial doubt slowly faded from his face. If there was a better bow in the world, it was clear now that he had never seen it. With two fingers around the bow string, he pulled back, taking an aiming shot, if only to test the strength required. That was enough for him, a scowl following.

"This? This might be good against a hare or small game—"

"She has downed an elk with such a bow," interrupted Halsedric.

"Where we a-goin', elk be the least 'o our problems, less'n you forgot. Out there be bigger game, an' sometimes it wears mail." Holding out the bow with a thrust, he continued, "This won't pierce mail."

"The wielder of that bow could put a dart through the eye of a raven on the wing at a hundred paces," Tulvgir answered. "Or have you forgotten already the previous demonstration of her skill?"

"She has no need to pierce mail," Halsedric countered. "Only spaces uncovered."

"A bow don't work in close quarters," Drahm mockingly spat back.

There was the sound of metal on metal and the rumble of cloth in the air, and before he knew it, Drahm was confronted by blade and dagger, grasped tightly in the hands of Herodiani.

Her actions clearly shocked the old guide as he took a step back. No longer angry, the clear blue eyes of Herodiani were now fierce and determined. The sword itself was made of bright steel, polished to a mirror shine with a single cutting edge, gripped tight by hands that knew how to hold a blade. Along the spine, etched with the skill of the artist, flowed runes and tangled depictions of vines and leaves. The blade was shorter than most he had ever seen, but the edge was still wicked sharp.

For a moment, Drahm was at a loss for words, visibly stunned and his eyes filled with doubt. It wasn't the weapons she bore, or the fierce will that lay behind those stunning blue eyes. It was the way she stood, and her confidence with the deadly implements she bore. A confidence of one who knew full well how to use those blades, borne of time and skill and the shedding of blood.

Halsedric said something to Herodiani in a flowing tongue that sounded beautiful and precise. With reluctance, she returned her weapons to their holders with the same deft skill that she drew them, before pulling her cloak back over her frame once more.

No longer as cynical and harsh as he was before, Drahm held out the bow.

Herodiani seized the weapon, the anger in her eyes no less abating.

"Convinced?" said Halsedric.

As if coming out of a stupor, Drahm straightened himself, his head turning this way and that, looking for something. His words came out soft, if not a little unsure. "Where be this fourth you spoke of?"

"There are only three," answered Halsedric.

"You told me provision for four."

Sniffing, Halsedric answered, "The Wodeman. He eats for two."

Sounding slightly insulted, Tulvgir grumbled deep in his throat before lifting his weapon and laying it on his shoulder. Turning, he left the gathering, heading toward the smoldering coals.

It was amusement enough for Drahm, who cracked a slight smile as his hands went to his hips.

Halsedric spoke. "Are you taking us where we need to go, or is our business complete? If not, return to me the gold I paid. I will find another guide."

Drahm's head stooped in thought for a moment before answering, "Aye. An' we best be off."

Breaking camp was a quick task, the trio having prepared to leave long before the guide met them. Saddlebags were thrown hastily on the horses as the others mounted their beasts. In all, there were four of the silvery white horses. They came on command, Halsedric calling them in the same flowing tongue he used when speaking to Herodiani. Fetching a pot from their gear, Halsedric filled it with water from a nearby stream and doused the fire. Like a nest of snakes, the coals hissed their displeasure, the steam rolling up in a bloom. It wasn't long before the horses were mounted and the company departed, moving in a single line.

The first leg of their journey was uneventful. In the lowlands west of the Dragonspires, the land was thick with trees and brush. Green and sometimes dark, the countryside was far from idyllic. Flies pestered rider and beast where the forest was thickest and the breeze could not keep them at bay. This only turned worse as they neared water, crossing over two separate wood bridges along their ride. There they took time to water the horses before continuing on.

At the bend of the road, they descended into the forest. Drahm guided them along game trails and sections of the forest where pines dominated, the ground buried in needles. In such places, brambles were few, ferns thigh-high dominated the terrain, shrouding what lay beneath them like a leafy fog of deep green.

Their first camp was made in the shadow of three old oaks and a crude structure made of timber and dirt. Nearby was a stream where water flowed from higher up on the mountain, clear and cold even in the growing summer heat. Drahm mentioned risking a fire. "Been here for years past. Nev'r seen a lick 'o trouble."

It took some time for Halsedric to convince Drahm to let the horses roam free. "These are Lenogala, the mounts of the Elanni. They need no hobbles or tying to posts. They will keep watch while we sleep and will shepherd your beasts as well as any stableman."

One eye cocked dubiously at the claim, the other eye closed and the lid creased, Drahm finally consented. His doubt about the Lenogala was never fully satisfied and his attention was constantly drawn to his horses during the night.

As they finished a meal of travel cakes and boiled rice, the guide took out his pipe and puffed contentedly. It was a crude pipe, the bowl roughly cut from some strange, dense root, a short stem poking out at a right angle from the bottom. Using a long dry twig they had collected as firewood, Drahm lit the weed he pressed into his bowl, sending large plumes of sweet-smelling smoke into the air. For a moment or two, he hummed a tune.

Bugs buzzed in and out of the smoke of the camp-fire, taking full advantage of the still air of the forest. The only salvation afforded the party were the bats that flapped and twirled overhead, feeding on the feast the camp presented them. Some dared come so close, they risked the hungry tongues of flame that rose from the burning wood.

"Old eyes," Drahm said, using the short stem of his pipe to point to Halsedric. He was leaning back against a stone, one leg out straight. Another leg was bent and its foot flat on the forest floor.

Halsedric sat cross-legged on the opposite side of the flame, his sword cradled in his lap, the blade nestled comfortably in its sheath. Tulvgir, for his part, was lain out on a blanket next to Drahm, head resting on a saddlebag, eyes staring up at the starry sky beyond the broken canopy of the trees.

"Couldn't place it ere now, but I know them eyes," Drahm continued, two fingers wrapped around the bowl, the end of the pipe stem making circles in the air as he spoke.

"What do you mean?" said Halsedric.

"Old eyes." Drahm's words slipped from his lips as if he struggled to explain his thoughts. "Eyes that seen battle. Eyes that seen blood bein' shed an' men dyin'. Them's that seen too much 'o the world. Old soldiers turned farmers an' forest men. A hard look an' faraway stare. Them's that drink their lives away each night with a smoking bowl. Old eyes, I call 'em."

Halsedric, for his part, made no sign of what he thought.

Taking a short draw, and releasing another plume into the air, Drahm continued. "What I can't figure is how one so young could have them eyes."

A slight snicker was heard from Tulvgir.

"What?"

"Those eyes are far older than you, old man," said Tulvgir with a grin.

Halsedric's eyes closed as a grumbling sigh bubbled up from deep within his chest. A rumble that signaled his deep discontent.

"You may as well tell him," answered Tulvgir. "There will be more questions in time."

"An' what might that be?" inquired Drahm, settling back, and putting the stem to his lips.

"You would not believe me if I told you," answered Halsedric.

"They never do," added Tulvgir with a curious smirk.

At this, Drahm shifted on the ground, "Tell me what?"

"No," Halsedric said with a slight shake of his head. Even Herodiani sniffed as she tended to her blade, kneeling on the ground next to him.

"What secrets are you keeping from me, boy?" The conversation now turned serious as Drahm's suspicions were aroused.

"That boy is far older than you, by a century or two," Tulvgir lazily replied.

"Oh, I see," Drahm answered, "'nother one of these Elanni?"

"Something like that," answered Halsedric.

"Something, but not one 'o them, say you?"

Head falling back and mouth open slightly, Halsedric inhaled, then exhaled noisily.

"Seen many a thing 'cross the years. What you say won't shock me none," Drahm answered.

To that, Tulvgir let out a loud snort.

"What?" Drahm said to Tulvgir, sounding offended.

After a short pause, Halsedric leaned to one side, snatched up a log, and cast it on the fire. The blaze erupted in a curtain of smoke and cinder, rising skyward and falling as dead ash to the ground around them.

"I lived in the time of the war between the prophets," Halsedric said in a low and serious voice.

"So you say," said Drahm, dubious.

"There, in the last battle, I was slain and restored to life by the Prophet Jalamil. Ever since, I have lived and labored, pursuant to the will of the Allfather, the one and only God that lingers in the West."

For a moment, Drahm sat there expressionless, staring at the youthful visage of the leader of the three, not quite understanding what he said. A second or two passed before his lips curled up and a long, wheezing laugh started. The old man bent forward as peals of laughter came out of him, eventually reclining as they decreased. Only when he was fit to speak did Drahm answer. He looked to Herodiani then to Tulvgir, expecting some sort of laughter, even the hint of a smile. Instead, all three were stone-faced and serious.

As his big toothy smile faded, Drahm piped up, a jovial tone dripping from his words. "You don't believe this jest?"

"'Tis true," Tulvgir answered.

In an instant, the laugher and the smile faded like an early morning mist, replaced by something angry, belligerent. "No man come back from the dead, by the gods!"

"There is but one God," Halsedric said, half answer, half scold.

"One God or many, none pass to death an' come back. Dead is dead," Drahm answered, trading one scold for another.

"It clearly is not," Herodiani answered, her speech rich with a rolling accent.

"Oh, so she talks, does she?"

"Yes, she knows your tongue," answered Halsedric. "She merely chooses to not use it."

Sour in his expression, his weathered features turning hard and hot, Drahm fell back with a huff. Pulling one long draw from his pipe, he expelled the smoke with a passive sort of defiance. "Madness, it 'tis," he groused low and contemptuously. "Should'a demanded more gold for my trouble."

CHAPTER 5

Three days they moved nearer to the mountains, with many days of travel already behind them. While a good portion of their trek was uneventful, crossing through open places nameless and mundane, once they pressed into the region of the Aranach, the mood of the party turned serious. Approaching the Torgiv meant moving through forests both thick and thin, seemingly absent of human occupation. Drahm was a skilled woodsman, that was clear. He knew which trails to take and those to avoid, when the road was their friend and when the wilds offered less risk. Caution, he made clear, was valued more than speed.

A good portion of their eastward trek traversed depressions in the earth; concavities where mists settled in the still mornings. These were mountain bogs where water collected and countless generations of seasonal plants grew, matured, and died back. Age after age of dead and compressed vegetation settled and sunk into otherwise higher elevations. Here the peat beneath their feat made the ground bounce and undulate as if they were walking upon mattresses buried by dirt. Long tracts all green, brown, and black where the stink of decay infiltrated their nostrils, and biting, stinging bugs harassed them every step forward. For the most part, they stayed on trails at higher elevations, where stag and wolf alike made narrow paths through the reeds and the muck. Tracts that were deceptively treacherous, each side screened by high grasses. Beyond that was swamp and muck, ready to trap and smother the unwary with grasping mud flats.

As one day merged into the next, the deciduous trees and fruiting brambles gave way to the sharp scent of pines and firs. Where brown leaves carpeted the forest floor, brittle needles and scattered cones became more and more frequent. Sometimes the bare rock broke through. Here, low junipers and thin mountain cedars clung to life with lichens and mosses, holding firm to fissures in the weathered and darkened stone. Now and again, one of them spied a mountain flower in the array of hard and hearty terrain, like a single shining star in a sky gone totally black. A small cluster of beauty in the harsh reality of the mountainous wilderness. Such things, however, were fleeting and rare.

At one point in their journey, it was Herodiani who halted the others with a whistle like that of a strange songbird. As if on command, the Lenogala stopped, their riders turning in the direction of the sound.

It took Drahm a moment before he understood what was actually going on. A cautious man, he rode over to the Elanni maid, pulling his pack horse with him. Approaching alongside, he halted and in a low voice asked, "Why do we stop?"

Her head turned and nodded to the right, somewhere ahead of them.

As the others moved in, Halsedric whispered, "What is it you hear?"

She shrugged her reply.

Looking around, Halsedric turned to Drahm and through squinting eyes said, "Dismount. Leave the horses. We investigate."

"Leave the horses?" Drahm's eyes went wide. "You mad?"

"The Lenogala," Halsedric answered, as if the name of the silvery-white horses was explanation enough.

One brow went up, the lines on his forehead leaving deep creases in his flesh. "Horse tendin' horse in the face `o peril? No. Leave the mountain man behind," he concluded with a nod of his head.

"I am no stableman," Tulvgir grumbled, his eyes narrowing in obvious irritation.

"Fine," answered Halsedric. "Tulvgir stays. The rest with me."

Slowly and quietly they dismounted as one of Drahm's beasts grumbled. Or perhaps it was Tulvgir. No one was truly sure.

A flattened bow in her hand, Herodiani wound her leg across the staff and pushed down while pulling up the bow string, setting the weapon ready for a shot. Unbinding her quiver from her bags, she slung the holder about her back, but not before pulling two arrows. These she clutched in her hand with her bow.

As the trio formed, they made off into the pine forest ahead, moving slowly. Needles crunched beneath the feet of Halsedric and Drahm. Herodiani, in stark contrast, moved with a silence and a grace that neither man possessed. At one point, one arrow she set in her teeth while the other she set into the bow string, preparing for a shot should the need arise.

Someone, or something else, was near. This became all the more evident the farther in they went. There was a rustling of the forest floor, faint at first, but incrementally louder with each careful footfall made. Before long, they came to a strand of red birch that acted as adequate cover for them all. Here their approach was painfully slow, as they dared not to step on the dry dead branches littering the ground. Snorting could be heard ahead of them alongside a steady, frantic rustling.

His axe at hand, Drahm stopped as he pulled a dagger from his belt. Removing the leather covering from the axe head, he tucked the device in his belt before continuing. His axe was an implement that was pitted and dark from years and years of use. The edge, however, remained bright, clean, and cunningly keen. A well-tended tool, even for moments such as these.

Hunched over and hoods up, each of them found a spot where they could gaze out at whatever it was that was creating the disturbance. From the gaps in the trunks they spied a small clearing where leaves and needles barely covered the stone beneath them. Laid out there, in dark leather and black mail, a body lay lifeless. As long as a man's forearm, straight horns colored black and brown shot out from a head covered with coarse black hair tangled and disheveled across the ground. The mottled green skin of its face was stained with a brackish fluid— its own blood by all accounts. A Yerch warrior by the looks of it, slain.

Its body twitched and rolled slightly as the thing that knelt over it went face-first into a wound, consuming the still flesh of its victim. Like the dead figure, this too had a mane of long, black hair, though thinning. The jaundiced skin beneath could barely be seen from the distance. Two stumps, charred black, were positioned at the fore of the head, a sad remainder of the horns that it once proudly owned. It growled and grunted as its head twisted and turned, a sickening wet sound following as its teeth tore at the sinewy flesh of its victim. One hand on the dead Yerch's belly, another holding firm its crown, the victor raised its head, tearing away a piece of flesh. It chewed nosily—a guttural sort of noise made by something starving as it slaked its gnawing hunger on the bounty before it.

"Yerch," Halsedric whispered.

Drahm pulled his attention away to look at the man standing next to him. It was a brief second, and one that hid what was to transpire next. Halsedric let out a shrill whistle, purposely.

Like a wolf suddenly surprised, the creature raised its head and stared straight ahead. Wide eyes fixed on the source of the noise, nonplussed. The stumps on his head were clear now, black and brown like that of the Yerch lying on the ground, but charred at the top. Sometime in the past, its horns were stricken off and cauterized by fire. Dark blood covered its lips and a good portion of the face, the sickly yellow hue of its skin showing through the streaks and splatters. Lips pulled back, dark flesh dangled like grim ribbons from its blackened, disorderly array of teeth, gleaming like fangs.

In that moment, a bow string snapped and a dart whooshed through the air, cutting the slight space between the two men. Through a narrow part on the birch branches, the missile flew straight and true, finding a home deep in the right eye socket of the victor in the grisly struggle.

Shocked and disturbed by the flight of the arrow, Drahm craned his neck around, his body following as the leaves on the forest floor spun beneath his feet. Behind him, in the corner of his eye, he thought he saw what looked to be the form of Herodiani, shrouded by what appeared to be forest. A hand came down, the bow she carried lowered with it. From her teeth, slim fingers plucked an arrow, setting it ready in the bow string.

A hand reached out and touched Drahm on the shoulder. His head snapped back, wide-eyed and afraid. He followed the length of the arm to Halsedric.

Calmly, Halsedric said, "Be still. And be patient."

This took a moment to register with the guide, his eyes filled with a nervous fascination.

Now there were two dead Yerch before them, but as one stopped moving, the other now twitched slightly, the head of the arrow having rent a path into its brain. Nerves fired aimlessly, simulating life where there was none. A white-fletched shaft stuck up from the wound of the dead creature, doing a little dance in the air as the body trembled. It was a troubling sight to see. Still, the pair waited and watched.

Long, tense seconds passed. Pulling back the fringes of her cloak, the lithe form of Herodiani appeared as if materializing out of thin air. Looking both ways, she slowly knelt at the head of her fallen prey.

"By the gods," Drahm muttered to himself.

Bow and arrow at the ready, Herodiani turned her head slowly about her, scanning the woods with her keen eyes, her sensitive ears straining at every sound made. After a time, her gaze found its way to where the others waited. With a single silent nod, she bid them approach.

Setting aside her bow and arrow, she pulled a dagger from her belt. Two quick thrusts to the creature's head ended the trembling, leaving the body still.

The Elanni maiden was still prying loose her arrow from the skull of her dead opponent as Drahm and Halsedric neared the grim scene.

Halsedric kicked at a sword, dagger, and a blood-stained rock that lay scattered on the ground, partly buried by dead pine needles and leaves. Drahm took to scouting the tracks of the two dead creatures, crouching at spots along the forest floor. He wandered as he tracked their movements from the forest fringe into the clearing.

Cutting a piece of cloth from the partially eaten Yerch, Herodiani went about cleaning the blood of her victim from her dagger and arrow. Once the dagger was back in its sheath, she took up her bow and rose to her feet, continuing to clean her prized missile.

Making his way back to the grim display, Halsedric investigated the creature felled by Herodiani's arrow. Pulling back the dome of the matted and greasy hair from its brow, his fingers traced the smooth skin of its face showing a mixture of curiosity and concern. The creature was thin and looked as if it had not eaten in days. With a drawn face, the ridges of its cheeks poked out sharp and deep beneath thinning skin. When Drahm approached, Halsedric stood up straight.

Herodiani milled about for a moment before letting the cloth drop and inspecting her arrow for damage.

"I've seen this kind `o creature before, jus' like that," Drahm said kicking at the shorn horns of the sallow-skinned Yerch. "Don't know what it means, tho'."

"He was an outcast," answered Halsedric. "One loses power to the other. Sometimes they are killed straightaway and eaten. Other times, to be more cruel, they cut off their horns and burn them at the base to keep them from returning. They are then left to fend for themselves."

Looking up and down the Yerch, Halsedric continued pointing at spots with his fingers. What was once mail was now little more than ragged remains of a shirt of metal rings, half corroded to uselessness. The rest of it was naked save for the skin of some unfortunate animal or animals that it used for a loincloth and partial cloak. "See here, how the armor is almost gone, and the gaunt limbs. This one was so desperate for food that it was willing to attack something far better armed and armored."

"An' won, it seems," said Drahm, spitting on the ground to his right, as if the scene left a foul taste in his mouth. After a moment, he turned slightly and pointed behind him. "Two there were. They struggled here. Ain't seen no more than a pair o' tracks, leadin' off away. Meanin' mayhaps others are some distance. Ain't hearin' nothin' tho'."

"What do you think we should do with the bodies?"

"Leave `em. Ain't worth the time to bury or burn."

"And what if more Yerch come looking for their lost comrade?"

Drahm looked up and cracked a dry smile. "Best then we be far, far away from here, aye?"

Halsedric was slow to move as Drahm turned away, choosing to inspect the armored Yerch that lost the duel. Crouching down near the head, he scanned the blood-spattered forehead much in the same way he did the first. There, as if branded into the flesh, he saw a mark—two rings connected one to the other. His brow furrowed at

46

the sight and his head tilted to one side. For a time, he remained, pondering the meaning of the mark.

"Aye! Best be off," Drahm scolded quietly. "No knowin' where the others are. What you lookin' at?"

"The yellow one. The one Herodiani slew? He is an ancient thing."

"What?"

"Ancient. Very old. And his brow is smooth." Halsedric's head nodded in the direction of the Yerch outcast. Pointing to the mark on the brow of the other he added, "This one has a mark. And the color is different. The old one is lighter, the other darker. I've seen them before, but never had the chance to inspect them close."

"Fine thing. But if we tarry here, I bet you'll see his fellows all up close an' such. So, I think it best we be off, aye?"

"Right," said Halsedric, distracted. Standing, he lingered for a moment and puzzled over the find before turning away.

CHAPTER 6

On the next day, spying a clearing up ahead, the party paused at the fringe of some dense wilderness. The trees too thick and low to ride, the group had been reduced to walking while the horses followed behind. Their path took them in a northerly direction, running parallel to the Horn of Torgiv. A road lay ahead of them, just beyond the ferns and brush. Drahm was the one who called for the halt, and patiently, he kept a sharp gaze on the open track ahead.

Halsedric commanded Herodiani to scout ahead.

"What you doing that for?" Drahm said angrily. "Sendin' a woman out ahead."

"Her eyes are better than yours," Halsedric answered. "And from here, we will see nothing."

Reluctant as he was, Drahm grumbled his consent and returned to the vigilance of his watch. "A few times I've seen folk moving up these roads towards the mountain," he said with a discontented whisper. "Strange folk. Not the type I want to see face to face, if'n you know what I mean."

Throwing her hood up and pulling her cloak around her, Herodiani stuffed her bow beneath the fold of her clothes before she paced silently away.

Drahm watched her intently, nervous and a bit curious. In a matter of moments, as if by magic, she faded into the forest as if she had melded with the wilds.

"Unnatural, if you ask me," he grumbled.

Long minutes passed by quietly. The sound of a distant raven counted down the time as it slowly ticked by. Half of the time, Drahm kept his eyes on the road. The remainder was spent watching the surrounding countryside, wondering where the slim woman perched. Despite his best efforts, he could find no trace of her.

"Nothing," said a high, sweet voice behind him. Drahm turned with a start, eyes bulging. Behind him, talking with Halsedric was Herodiani, bow in hand and hood back, as if she had never left. His gaze said it all. How?

Slowly they parted from the wood, moving onto the road. Crude, cracked stone paved the track, the edges of it overgrown by tall weeds, junipers, and saplings. Here, they mounted up and moved forward in a single line, Drahm at the front, Halsedric just behind with one horse tied to his saddle. Tulvgir tended to the other horse Drahm had brought to bear their supplies. Holding far to the rear of their column, the Elanni maiden sat astride her silvery-white mount, keeping watch on the road when time and consequence allowed.

Before them loomed the ominous form of the Horn of Torgiv. It was an unusually tall peak flattened and sheared on the southern face, giving a bowed appearance. A great whitecap graced the tips, while the remainder of the peak was a drab gray stone. One of the largest of the range, it was intimidating even from afar, giving off an ominous allure.

Called the Dragonspires by men, the eastern mountains had a history that was steeped in mystery and superstition. As the name denoted, this hard and desolate place is said to be where dragons roamed, praying on the unwary. Yerch certainly called these mountains home, as well as the heartier breeds of Morgurs, the great stinking beasts of ancient lore. Few good things came from these mountains. Wodemen mined the wealth beneath the peaks, though the dangers they faced were a daily concern. Bandits were said to find shelter in hidden holds somewhere among the peaks. It was an apt place for evil to find refuge, for the history of this range spans long into ancient memory, and little of it good.

Before long, they stopped at a pair of statues that loomed up before them on both sides of the road. Like great totems of gray granite, weathered by time and the elements, they were pitted, pieces having cracked and fallen away. Moss clung to the crevices, dried, and took on a pale, sickly hue. Carved into the stone of each was a figure like that of a man, head down, hood shrouding the features of what lay beneath. Yet, before them, crossed like the hands of a corpse, fingers long and tipped with sharp nails curled like talons of some terrible creature. In many ways, they looked like a pair of vultures perched atop a branch, staring down at their dying prey, waiting patiently to pick the bones of the fallen.

As grim as these stone guardians were, what lay at their base was enough to cause even Herodiani to gasp when her eyes beheld it. Dark smears at the feet of the sentinels, the rock here was stained by what Halsedric concluded was blood left to bake and burn into the stone. At the feet of the columns rested a tangled array of bones, assumed to be those of sacrificed animals. Yet on closer inspection, he discovered the skull of a man and the twin horns of a Yerch thrusting upward from the gray and ivory piles.

"Enough to chill the bones," Drahm said in response to the sound of the Elanni.

"A place of sacrifice?" inquired Tulvgir, looking around at the sight.

"Aye," answered Drahm with a nod. "A sacrifice for passage, methinks. Tho' I must admit, I'm not likely to go a-askin' what it all means."

"And what is your custom?" said Halsedric to Drahm.

"Me? None. Tho' I leave it to those I guide to make their own mind on th' matter."

Halsedric dismounted and approached the statue to his right, the stone chips grinding and scraping together with each footfall. He halted at the edge where the bones were piled around the base. There, he looked up into the dark space of the hood, wondering if anything existed past the shadows. These statues were as much markers as they were a statement. They heralded a warning of what lay beyond. That the land past their silent watch was a place poorly suited for the timid or cautious.

"Naught lives at their feet," said Tulvgir.

"What say you?" Herodiani said, her head turning towards the Wodeman.

A meaty finger pointed to the ground as Tulvgir spoke. "The ground. Where there was grass and green? The ground here is bare all the way to the trees."

Heads collectively turned this way and that, and as Wodeman observed, not a single green thing lived around the base of either statue for at least thirty feet.

Maybe some dried leaves of an autumn past, or pine needles turned brown and fragile, but life was absent in the stone. As if any living green thing could not be tolerated in their presence, the life wicked away.

Ominously, a raven croaked in the distance and the sun darkened as if the stone wardens sucked the very light from the sky.

"What comes next?" said Halsedric, his eyes never parting from the statue before him.

"Past them we go, a mile methinks," Drahm replied. "Then into the forest and make camp. After that, we part."

"Part?" The revelation was enough for Halsedric to turn suddenly. "You are paid to deliver us here and back."

"Aye," Drahm answered Halsedric, his chin high. "Here I have brought you, an' at camp I'll wait. I'll go no further into this place. That's your burden, not mine. Six days you have. Come the morn' on the seventh, I'll be off."

"And how far to the tomb?" Tulvgir's eyes barely left the statues. The threat and dread they stirred in him both repulsed and demanded his attentions. Like a terrible scene of carnage that horrified and amazed all at once.

"From camp? Two leagues I reckon, maybe less. No more than two hours on a quick march."

"And I suppose you expect us to settle our account at camp?" said Halsedric.

"Aye," Drahm nodded. "No sense tryin' to collect my fee from the dead."

"And of the Yerch?" asked Tulvgir.

With a chuckle that could drain the strength from even the boldest of men, Drahm answered, "No Yerch.

Nothin' fool enough to tarry here. Least whiles none I ever seen in all the years I've been a-takin' treasure huntin' fools to this place."

"I like that naught. Not one bit," growled Tulvgir.

"An' I don't likes some stubby mountain man questionin' my honor," Drahm testily shot back.

"Enough," Halsedric commanded. Without another word, he turned back to one of the statues. He began to kick away the bones until he had cleared a space deep enough where he could reach out and touch the base. The bleached and weathered shafts and fragments made a hollow clacking as he disturbed their rest. Pulling his dagger from his belt, he set the tip of it to the fleshy part of his palm. Dragging the blade across his skin, he made a gash until blood welled up and pooled in his hand.

"What are you doing?" Herodiani said alarmed. Her horse grumbled and shifted forward in response to her cries.

Without explanation, Halsedric drew his hand across the stone of the statue, leaving a smear of blood on the graven pillar. As he did, the trail of his blood began to bubble, smoke, and spit as if it were oil poured into a pan left on the stove until over-hot.

"Find me a bandage," Halsedric said as he pulled back from the statue, scanning the wound of his hand. "I need to bind the wound."

Herodiani dismounted as the others watched the blood bubble and hiss on the stone. Tulvgir's eyes opened wide, and Drahm's mouth fell open. None of them knew what to make of what they spied.

Halsedric turned and made his way back to his horse. "Let us leave this foul place and make camp. We strike out for the tomb come dawn."

"And what then?" spoke Herodiani as she rifled through her bags looking for something to use as a bandage. "How will we find the place we seek?"

"This here path leads to a road. You'll see it soon enough. Well mark'd it 'tis," answered Drahm. "No need for a guide. You can find it easily. And there'll be no mistakin' the land it takes you to."

"What say you?" said Tulvgir.

With a wry smile and knowing look, Drahm spoke through a laugh. "You'll see. Oh, you shall see."

CHAPTER 7

Unwrapping his wounded hand, Halsedric flexed and relaxed his fingers, inspecting the wound by the firelight. The gash that bled so openly and easily only a few hours before was little more than a thin line of red, dotted and decorated by the rust-colored stains of blood on his palm. Fingers moved and danced as he tested the scar.

Next to him, Drahm made himself a fine resting place, his back against a pile of saddlebags and gear, his axe and bow nearby. Feet towards the fire, he had a dagger that he used to cut through a brown hunk of something in his hand. Halsedric had seen it before in his travels—Trapper's Bread. A thick, dense loaf made from whatever was available, preserved in fat or honey, and pressed like a cake. Peeling off a thick slice, Drahm held it pinched against the blade with his thumb as he lifted it to his mouth.

Herodiani was in the wilds, somewhere perched on a tree, keeping watch over the others. Tulvgir snoozed carelessly on the ground on the opposite side of the fire. Somewhere outside of the fire's light, the horses milled about, making little sound in the still of the growing night.

Chewing, Drahm took the occasion to look over at Halsedric. Seeing a wad of bloodstained cloth in Halsedric's hand, he sat up to get a better look at the wound.

"I can make a mash for that, if'n you need," said Drahm, motioning with his dagger.

Turning slightly to his left, Halsedric held up the wounded hand for the grizzled guide to see.

Drahm squinted for a moment, his eyes focusing in the dim amber glow of the campfire. There, hidden in the shadows and light, he saw how the wound was near healed. "By the gods," Drahm muttered, stunned.

"There is but one God," Halsedric said as he pulled the hand away.

"I can't believe my eyes."

Halsedric turned back, continuing to flex his fingers.

"An' this God of yours grants you th' power to heal?" Drahm turned suddenly curious.

"A consequence of my condition."

Silence followed, the crackling of the fire and Tulvgir's snoring being the only sounds that filled the night. The wilderness was often a quiet place, even at this time. Here it was doubly so. The baying of wolves and the retort of wild dogs were often heard when the moon rose high. Insects calling out, and the screech of a distant owl all familiar as the world slept. But this night and in this place, all was frightfully still.

"Bein' dead?"

"Raised," answered Halsedric. "Not dead."

"An' what other surprises have you?"

His wounded hand balled into a fist, he laid his arm against his knee. Halsedric was slow to answer. "Strength of limb. Quick with a blade, quicker than most. I have a vigor unmatched by any mortal."

Halsedric inhaled deeply as the guide took another bite of his meal. "The air is thick here. I would think that being up here in the heights, it might be thinner. Clearer."

"Just noticin' it?"

"Why?"

"Once you pass them statues, somethin' haunts this land. Repels us. Thick air is where it starts, like th' wet air of the lowlands. Where's that maiden of yours?"

"Keeping watch," replied Halsedric as he stared at his hand. Letting it fall, he added, "The Elanni have no need for sleep. It makes her a good watchman as we rest."

"The dead have need for sleep, aye?" Drahm chuckled quietly, having amused himself.

"Do you still doubt my story, old man?" said Halsedric. He pushed himself back from the fire.

"Answer me this," Drahm piped up, "Was it your God who saved you from a dagger blow in th' back?"

Halsedric turned his head slightly.

"Aye, I saw the stain, an' the stitchin' on your vest."

"Part of the same condition, I suppose," answered Halsedric.

"A cut like that leaves a man dead, lessin' luck be with 'em. I hear them wizards have powers that bring a man back from th' dead. You a wizard?"

"No," replied Halsedric with a shake of his head. "And the wizards you speak of, they are sent by the same God. He that dwells in the West."

"An' them dark wizards I hear tell bein' about?"

Halsedric sniffed a laugh.

"Aye?"

Halsedric was quick to change the subject. "What do you know of the place we seek?"

"I know enough to venture no further than here. An' I know there ain't no gold up in that wretched place, least whiles none worth dyin' for." Drahm laid the dagger in his lap as well as the chunk of the loaf he intended to eat. Taking a cloth that lay neatly at his side, he started to wrap his rations once more and ready their return to a saddlebag.

"Gold is not what we seek."

"As you say. But somethin' is up there that you're willin' to risk life an' limb."

"What do you know of the Great War?"

Drahm paused his activity and pondered the question. "Meanin' the one with them prophets and all?"

"No. The one before."

Setting down the wrapped loaf, Drahm thought on the question again. "Don't reckon no war worth rememberin'."

"Not surprising," Halsedric said with a sigh. "It ended a long, long time ago. Hundreds of years before I was born, I think. A long and terrible affair where the dead remain unnumbered and where the face of the world was changed."

"Aye," Drahm said with a nod. "I heard a few of them legends, when a traveler or two were seekin' a coin or free mug. But them legends ain't nothin' but tall tales, made taller for silver, if'n you know what I mean."

"Legends oft come from history. Yet this history is one best forgotten. Herodiani was born in the waning days of that terrible time. And it formed the Great Inland Sea."

"The Sorrowin' Sea, you mean?"

Halsedric turned his head slightly towards Drahm. "How do you think it got that name? By the many dead that lay in its depths. The grand might of an ancient host, a terrible host that threatened to destroy all that is good and noble. Crushed by foundering earth and sunk beneath the waves. What we seek is from that war." Halsedric's gaze returned to the shimmering coals and licking flames of their campfire. "A dark conjurer out of the east whose might and dark sorceries surpassed the greatest Elanni lord or hero of the Heavenly Host."

"An' what happened to him?" said Drahm, his attention fixed intently on the man sitting next to him.

"Accounts recall that he was slain, if such things can truly be slain. What we seek is his tomb."

"To what end?"

Halsedric paused for a moment. "To ensure that whatever was sealed away in that stony crypt remains within. There have been growing rumors of a dark presence somewhere in the east of the world. Strange things afoot. Devotees to a dark and secretive cult. It took me some time to uncover this place, for few then knew of its location. Fewer still ever recorded where it lay."

Craning his neck full around in an attempt to look Drahm in the eye, Halsedric added, "Of all the guides who knew these lands, you were the only one who would take us to this place. So it was we sought you out, for what it matters."

"An' that's all you seek?"

"For the most, yes," answered Halsedric with a purposeful nod.

"For th' most?"

"That and whatever secrets we find within. He was not the only one interred within that dread place. Two of his generals as well. They may be naught but bones and dust, but other things may have been entombed with them."

"Such as?"

Halsedric shrugged. "Of that I know naught. Perhaps chronicles preserved by dry stone, perhaps nothing. It took long enough to piece together the few clues to where this place lay."

As Halsedric turned his head away, Drahm went about picking up his knife, his nightly meal, and the bundled loaf. Shifting to his side, he returned the loaf to one of his bags. "Sendin' th' dead, to chase th' dead," he said just above a mutter.

"What was that?"

It was some time before Drahm answered, turning back and setting himself upright against his gear. "I said, sendin' th' dead to chase th' dead. You bein' once dead an' all."

"Once dead, but restored."

"So say you."

Looking Drahm in the eye once more, Halsedric said, "Even after all you have seen, you do not believe?"

Drahm answered, "I've had my time followin' after gods. Th' prayers and th' tributes. From that I learned but one thing. Gods are fickle. More interested in sacrifice an' worship, than those followin' after. Aye, I prayed when I was young. An' what was it I got? Nothin' but trial an' trouble."

"I guess that depends on what gods you follow after."

"Meanin' what?"

"What gods did you follow? The Four?"

"I should say not," Drahm exclaimed, sitting up as if he had been insulted. "The old gods. Not them bloody things they follow in th' south."

"New gods or old, neither can hear your petitions. Those that are new act in rebellion to the Allfather. The old gods of which you speak were merely the fabrication of men seeking to explain the seasons and the changes in the world. Something to give meaning and purpose for what they could not explain."

"A God that makes rebels?" Drahm laughed. "He don't sound so high an' mighty to me."

"And yet, you speak to one who was once dead, and still lives. One whose wounds heal over the course of a night and whose flesh does not falter with dart or blade."

"An' if I bend th' knee to this God of yours, I too can expect a life nev'r endin'?" With a snickering shake of his head, Drahm added, "I heard tell lots of you be-lievin' types pinned to th' trees of the Cathars, screamin' out their last. None 'o them came back from th' black-ness of death, I'll wager. They died just like any that bent th' knee to old gods or th' Four. So, tell me, friend, what does your God offer me that th' others don't?"

"Salvation."

"Ho, salvation is it?" Eyes wide as saucers, and with mocking tones, Drahm waved his dagger at Halsedric.

"Eternal life," answered Halsedric.

"Like you?"

"Not like me," Halsedric said patiently. "Men meas-ure life in the span of years. To the Allfather, time has no meaning."

"Right then," Drahm said with a smirk. "Only end-less years for a few, then."

"No." Halsedric shook his head. "Even I will die, in time. No one born of mortal flesh lives forever. There will come a time, however, when this world comes to an end. It is then the faithful will be raised. Not in a day, or a year, or a thousand, thousand years."

"Does little for me now. An' little for you."

"Yet it costs you nothing to simply believe," replied Halsedric patiently.

"What's that?"

"Tell me, friend, what does it cost you to merely believe? A few words said in prayer. To live a life that helps others? Just as you risk yours to bring us here?"

"That's diff'rnt," grumbled Drahm with a slight scowl. "I go for gold."

Head tilting to one side, Halsedric cast a dubious glare at the elder guide. "Gold that could more easily be gained by merely letting Jethlo know where we were camped, as well as our numbers."

Not having a ready answer, Drahm snorted and his hand waved Halsedric away.

The conversation coming to a sudden end, Halsedric's eyes became preoccupied with the fire. Drahm bit another mouthful of his slice of loaf.

"Tell me, Drahm, what would it take for you to believe?"

There was a chuckle as one side of Drahm's mouth lifted at the question.

"What?" said Halsedric.

"If'n you don't come a-runnin' back from that place as pale as the ghosts, then mayhaps you returnin' alive might."

Halsedric thought on this for a while. "Running back?"

"Aye."

"From what?"

"You'll see, soon enough," Drahm answered with a terrible cackle. "Soon enough."

CHAPTER 8

As cryptic as it was, the warning of the guide made itself known within the span of a mile. Vegetation that was once thick and green became sparse, withered. Verdant forest changed as if the color of the world was somehow wicked away—brown, gray, and black dominating their view. Even the moss that clung tenaciously to trees and brittle stone seemed withered and dried. The life contained within all but absent, the remains desiccated. Before long, bare branches absent leaves or needles remained, the husks of the trees rent and splintered, yielding to nature. The air grew still and soundless save for the whispers and rumors of the wind. That and the jarring call of the occasional raven, the only creature bold or foolish enough to brave these accursed grounds.

Drahm was correct. The path was clear to see, for nothing grew upon it. A stony road, whose passage led them into a landscape that looked like something from another world. Even the occasional gusts of wind did little to lighten the heavy, oppressive air that surrounded them. Something thick pressing down on them with each step forward, as if some unseen will was trying to keep them away.

Tulvgir was quick to note what they all thought. "I have heard legends from the Algonkin, who come to trade with us from time to time. In their stories, they talk of cursed places such as this. Where the underworld spills out into realms of the living. Ground where no living thing should tread."

"Legends, only," Halsedric said in an offhand way.

"Yet, you cannot deny that there is more death here than life."

"Let us not linger here in speculation. We have a task to attend," answered Halsedric.

A steep incline led upwards to a landing, a hard trail made all the more treacherous by a bed of shattered rock beneath their feet. Halsedric's feet slipped at times, the grate and crunch of hard points of granite grinding and shifting. The dust of stony particulate billowed up like spores from hidden mushrooms. Each footfall threatened to give way, sending him sliding downwards and taking the others with him. Dead branches aided their passing, though still with great risk. The wood gone brittle and gray, the weaker limbs often cracked or disintegrated in their hands. Only when they reached the top did they stop and marvel in a strange sort of horror of the landscape before them.

Stone dust clung to their clothes as if the ground itself took a part in burying them, one thin layer of dust at a time. Gray clouds erupted around them as they tried their best to bat the stone dust from their garments. The noise they made lessened over time, each stopping as their gaze caught the scenery around them. Dozens of mounds chaotically dotted the stony base of the angry mountain peak, barrows of the dead. Before them were heaps of piled stone near the height of a man, rising up like warts on some sleeping creature. Between each lay a gap, leaving serpentine paths up a shallow rise. At the end of the paths awaited a crooked, crude stair.

Like a worm that clung tenaciously to an angled and jagged rock face, the stair wound up the mountain, ending at a ledge jutting out from a triangular fissure in a sheer stone face. It was as Drahm mentioned, though a few details remained absent.

Concern overtook them all, Herodiani being the most affected. Her bright blue eyes opened wide, faced with a staggering field of death and decay, an immortal standing at the fringe of a vast graveyard. It was a grim view of the mortality of men. Death was a subject foreign to her kind and something she scarce considered.

"How many are there?" she asked in an awed whisper.

"Unknown," Halsedric answered. "Too many to stop and count."

"Who are they?"

"Followers, no doubt," Tulvgir said.

"Followers? It was difficult enough to find this place."

"Toudenress."

"What say you?" said Herodiani.

"Lord of the Dead," Halsedric answered. "In the tongue of the Wodemen."

"Lord of Bones, to be more precise," Tulvgir added. "Though Lord of the Dead is quite close. There is a legend that such a devil existed in these parts. A few tall tales from miners and wanderers who frequent these spires." He paused for a moment, his eyes shifting this way and that. When he spoke again, his words were furtive and uncertain. "At least we believed it only a legend."

"I did not know he had followers," said Herodiani, her attention drawn once more to the mounds that dotted the land and rise before them.

Halsedric pulled up the fringe of his cape and continued to bat away the dust that tenaciously clung there. "When he was slain, he and his lieutenants were buried here in secret. No doubt, the legend of his might persisted."

He stopped his activity for a moment, pausing for thought. "A cult, I think. I heard rumors of such. Then again, there are always rumors of dark things."

"So, you think they are followers entombed within the barrows?" said Tulvgir.

Halsedric dropped his cloak and clapped his hands clean, turning his head away briefly so as not to breathe in the granite particles. Face pinched, he coughed once before opening a single eye. "Perhaps. Perhaps those that escaped being slain in the first war? Later generations venerating some dark god? Only the Allfather knows for certain."

Bending down, Tulvgir picked up a few of the cracked and jagged stones at his feet. He moved them about in his fingers, inspecting them before carelessly tossing them aside. "Drab granite. Good for building walls, but little else. There are places north of here that will yield greater gains."

"Is this cursed ground?" Herodiani asked of Halsedric.

"We shall see," he answered. Throwing back his cloak, he grasped the hilt of his sword and pulled it free of its scabbard. At once, the shining metal, etched with runes along the spine, hummed, and changed its glow to that of a red-hot brand. Colored flames erupted around the steel, dancing along its edges—orange, yellow, red, and green. The weapon igniting was enough to cause a start in the other two, both of them leaning back slightly.

"I do not think I will ever be accustomed to that," Tulvgir said with a shake of his head.

Turning the blade down, Halsedric thrust the tip of his sword into the loose stone with little effect – at first. Halsedric's sharp gray eyes watched intently. Soon, the stones twitched and popped like dried corn in a hot skillet, telling him all he needed to know. Pulling out the blade, he promptly returned it to its holder where it hung, lashed around his shoulders.

This was an unholy place. There was no doubt of that now. As if whatever contained beneath the stone of the mountain spilled out like poison from the root. Halsedric's companions breathed uneasily, each looking to the other with anxious eyes.

"Let us keep moving," Halsedric said as he pulled the fringe of his cloak back over the hilt of his sword. "We accomplish nothing standing here prattling on about rumors and legends while the daylight wanes."

Of the three, only Halsedric seemed the most unaffected by the barrows. As he took the lead, the others followed behind, heads down at times, sometimes looking sidelong at the stony mounds. Loose stone ground and creaked beneath the heels of their boots, small tufts of dust rising and falling with each footfall. Herodiani eyed the crude constructions nervously, as if she fully expected something from beneath the loose stone heaps to reach out and grab her. Hidden hands breaking through stone and pulling her into the dead space within.

The skin beneath the thick hair of Tulvgir itched, standing up on the back his head with anxious despair. With each step forward, the hatred of this place grew in their hearts and minds. Sorcery, perhaps. Or perhaps the vague reminder that mortality was simply a sword stroke away.

There were minor details that distinguished one tomb from the next. Some were merely piles of broken stone, set in a natural heap. Others were larger, with cut posts and beams that formed a simple entrance, over which was set a rectangular stone to close the gap. The farther in they moved, the more elaborate the barrows became, some sporting runes carved into the cut stone, weathered by time and nature. Graven images decorated some. Images carved either into the face of the stone doorways or as statues like horrid guardians, left to protect those interred within. Near the stair, however, the largest were erected, rising the height of a man and a half. Here the inscriptions were the most worn, as if nature itself tried to blot away any sign of who or what was housed within. Men of prominence, perhaps, if it were men that actually lay inside. Most had capstones that sealed their entrances, cracked in places, broken at their edges.

The seals that once held the capstones in place had fallen away long ago. Some of the capstones here were greatly weathered, broken in places, the darkened interiors exposed to the elements. The curiosity to look within was held in check by the dread of what they might find. Even the daylight, diffused beneath the canopy of thick clouds overhead, offered no hope or comfort among the tombs of the wicked.

At the stairway, they looked up, desiring to go forward, yet hating the very notion of continuing on. A curiously cold wind blew and a howl went up among the tombs, only to settle back into silence once more. A raven fluttered down and rested atop one of the mounds. As long or longer than a barnyard hen, it was an imposing creature despite its size. Head cocked to one side, it eyed the trio before barking at them twice. The jarring croak was enough for the three to turn their heads with a snap.

For a time, Halsedric studied the creature as its head twitched and turned, one dark eye seemingly fixed on him. It barked again, harsh and threatening, its wings puffed out before the feathers slowly settled. Something about it caught and kept his rapt attention, far beyond that of any other creature of the air. The hair on the back of his head stood up and the tips of his fingers itched.

With a slow turn of the head, he looked at Herodiani and calmly commanded, "Kill it."

An unnerving caw and the flurry of feathers were heard immediately after, the black bird taking to the air. The coincidence not lost on Halsedric, his eyes followed the bird as it lifted itself from the mound and pushed to higher climbs.

Herodiani put arrow to bow string, and like the keen huntress she was, followed the flight of the crow. Her actions quick, the bow string snapping, the fletching of her dart hissed as it cut the air. The path of the projectile was on an undeniable course to strike the creature dead in the center of its chest.

At the last moment, the bird turned at an impossible angle. The arrow passed by, clipping only a few of the jet-black tail feathers, leaving small remnants to float out and down, back to the earth in their own good time.

For a time, the three adventurers stood there looking up in amazement, barely able to believe what their eyes had seen. The raven let out one last mocking croak as it disappeared like a black smudge into the leaden horizon. Both Tulvgir and Halsedric turned their attention to the Elanni maiden, befuddled and disconcerted. She never missed. Not even a single time.

Slow and purposeful, Herodiani inspected her bow and tested the tension of her string. Looking up to meet the expectant gaze of her comrades, her lips moved soundless, words unable to provide an explanation.

Once more, the echo of that dreaded raven cawed in the distance. One last parting protest and curse.

"I hate this place," Herodiani was heard to say.

"Hate is not a strong enough word," Tulvgir answered.

The stair itself was narrow and wound up the cliff face, carved from the dreadful stone itself. At the base, Halsedric looked down and saw something partially covered by the rubble. Kneeling, he took up the object with his fingers, drawing it out from the cracked debris that covered it. It was a dagger. The blade was bent and deeply embedded with rust, the cross-guard that was once brass now encrusted with a greenish patina. The leather that covered the handle was decayed and tattered, the shaved bone that made the handle now gray and cracked.

He stood up swiftly and held it up for the others to see.

"Adventurers," said Tulvgir.

"Fleeing adventurers," answered Halsedric as he tossed the implement away.

Ascending the narrow stair was their next trial. It was only less perilous than climbing the cliff face itself. The carven steps were uneven and often broken at the edges, worn by time and the elements. Halsedric spent part of the climb hunched over, keeping his center of gravity low, grasping at handholds where he could find them. Each step he eyed with trepidation, making sure the ground was solid beneath his feet. Small chips from cracked edges fell away, clicking and cracking as they plummeted into the field of tombs below. It was a not so subtle reminder of how the whole of this wretched place was bent on killing the foolish and unwary.

The others had less of a struggle. The deftness of the Elanni was a boon to Herodiani, her silent footfalls finding sure ground as she held fast to the wall of the stone face. Tulvgir, skilled in traversing stony passages of less structure and definition, found no toil in his rise to the top. Whether they found Halsedric's clumsy ascent comical, none dare show it. Part of this was their respect for the man and his skills. The remainder was due to each having a vigilant eye on the ground below them; the many tombs of the dead that lay silent and foreboding below.

Only as they reached the narrow ledge at the top did they all turn and look back from whence they came. The sight was inexplicable to their senses, the pause and awe returning as they first laid eyes on this damnable spot. Great lumps dotted the ground like the obscene bumps on some great leprous beast buried in the drab stone of the mountainside.

In unpracticed unison, they turned toward the dark crevice that split the mountain face. A dim, foreboding place rent into the mountain where their final destination lay.

"Ready the lantern," Halsedric said as they stared into the deepening dark. "I require aid, dressing in my surcoat."

CHAPTER 9

Tulvgir cracked two of the crystals together before dumping them into the holder of the brass lantern. The hinge squeaked as he closed the door, the latch making a hollow metallic click. The yellow-orange light proved a poor substitute for the sun in the dark space where they sheltered, but it was nonetheless welcome.

Such was the way the Wodemen lit their way in their dark halls of stone. They were masters at using the wonders of the earth as their playthings, their crystals of light being among them. From whence the crystals came or how they were discovered was a secret of the mountain folk, and vigilantly guarded.

The light stones were one of the many benefits to having Tulvgir in his company. Oil burned and was expended. Torches burned briefly, and many were needed for deep excursions into the depths of the earth. Candles dripped wax and were too easily extinguished. Aside from the violent hammering required to light them, the stones on Tulvgir's lamp lasted longer and were brighter than any of the others.

A light rain began to fall just outside of the split in the stone. Halsedric noted each wet spot form on the ledge as the Wodeman prepared his lamp.

"Thank the Allfather we did not have to climb in the rain," Halsedric said in half-reverent tones. His pack and his cloak lay in a heap on the leveled stone floor. Herodiani had helped him lay the surcoat over his frame. Lifting it such that his head fit through the hole, Halsedric stooped while she draped the cloth over him. The fabric of the garment covered him both front and back.

There was not much to the surcoat. A heavy white cloth whose previous stains had been bleached away, it was trimmed with gold stitching along the hem. Immaculate gold letters were embroidered on the chest, a declaration that none of them knew or could read.

"I don't see why you need to wear that here," Tulvgir said as he opened the iris of the lamp, the light of the crystals flooding the dark space, pushing back the shadows. "What purpose does it serve here? In this dismal place?"

"Have you not read the words of the Prophet Jalamil?" said Halsedric with a slight curve on his lip. He almost looked amused by the Wodeman's question.

"Prophets are for men."

"Wise words are for all to heed," Herodiani answered as she stepped back from Halsedric, giving him room to put on his belt. "It does not matter from whence such wisdom stems."

Tulvgir grunted as he stood, lamp in hand. The light of it bounced and danced haphazardly in that triangular arch of rock.

"Thy word is thine breastplate and shield. That I shall brave the slings of thine enemies, unhurt and unbowed." Halsedric's head lifted slightly as he recalled the phrase from memory, his words purposeful and reverent.

"A good coat of mail would do the same," answered Tulvgir.

"Blasphemous words do not help us here," Herodiani warned as she stooped to take up Halsedric's sword, being careful to grasp the weapon by its sheath.

Halsedric chuckled softly. "Faith is a hard thing to come by in places such as these. I think a few ill-said words can be forgiven considering where we stand."

Head tilting to the side, Tulvgir shone the light on the golden lettering that emblazoned Halsedric's breast. The script was fluid, almost beautiful as he eyed each character. "Have you ever uncovered what it says?"

"No." Halsedric's head bowed as he fastened the belt around his waist and tied it snugly, leaving the end to dangle down the front of him. "It matters little to me."

With a grunt, Tulvgir turned the light on the darkened passage before them, his eyes seeing something vague at the end. He breathed deeply and let out a long wavering sigh. Kneeling slightly, he took up the handle of his weapon, clutching it tightly in his strong fingers. His hands were muscled and riddled with veins. His palms were as coarse and as tough as rawhide, the consequence of long years working with wood and stone. The light of the lamp danced in the peaked and cragged space whose vault came to a sharp pointed tip of a triangle. He let out a deep, throaty "harumph" as he inspected the construction.

"The sides were left rough and uneven, though I see no tooling anywhere."

"Do not stray too far without us," Halsedric warned.

After slinging the strap that held his sword about his shoulder, Halsedric pulled his cloak around him, clasped it securely with a bronze buckle. Herodiani was quick to take up her bow from behind, throwing back the hem of her cloak before plucking an arrow from her quiver. This she set into the bowstring of her weapon should the need arise.

Forward they moved in unison into the dark fissure. Feet scraped against cold stone, the sound of it seeming hollow in that space. The light of the lamp darted from one spot to the next as Tulvgir explored their environs, noting each feature wordlessly. Yet the one thing that kept his attention the most was the back of the hallway, which slowly came into view. Despite the rough walls, the floor was smooth, as was the wall they were approaching. But as the light revealed what lay at the end, Halsedric sighed and his throat rumbled with displeasure.

The wall ahead was smooth, even and gray, the middle of it looking as if it had been blasted away. Roughly rectangular in shape, the hole itself was just wide enough for a man to squeeze by. What lay beyond was utter black.

"This is ill news," Halsedric said. "The first ward has been breached."

"And how many wards—" asked Tulvgir.

"I know of four. Two here on the entrance. Another that seals the crypt. A fourth on the box in which he was contained," answered Halsedric.

Approaching with caution, they stopped at the wall. Setting down his mace, Tulvgir took time to inspect the stone, running his hand along the broken edges, his fingers rubbing at some blackened areas at the center of the breech. The remainder of the time, his hand traced a faint line that ran parallel to the crude doorway. He hummed, puzzled as he moved to inspect the other side, finding something similar. Stone chips ground beneath his feet as he moved.

"What do you see?" said Halsedric.

Stepping back, Tulvgir nearly fell as some of the stone shifted beneath his feet. The light from his lamp leapt spastically as he recovered and he kicked away some of the pebbles that threatened to toss him on his backside. He cursed at them low in his native tongue before looking up and checking his lamp. As reason returned to him, he stared at the blank stone wall, eyeing a single vertical line.

"'Tis as if the stone here was welded. Like the steel of a blade reforged and remade."

"Cunningly fitted," remarked Halsedric.

"No," replied Tulvgir, turning slightly and looking up. "The stone here is knitted. 'Tis a single stone, but the grain differs on each side. I know of none among my kind with such skill."

As his attention returned to the stone face before him, the fingers of his free hand moved to his beard, stroking the hairs of it as he wondered silently.

At first, Halsedric was quiet, letting the Wodeman ponder. However, he moved to more pressing matters.

"And of the breech?"

"The breech?" parroted Tulvgir, his eyes not leaving the seam, nor wandering from the puzzle that it presented to him. "Scorching in the center means fire, and there are marks from a pick there too. Fire can be used to weaken stone, but such a fire would be built at the base and not in the center where the dark marks are placed. If there was a fire or a blast, it would be at the center. Perhaps a man whose pick struck the stone."

"The ward," added Halsedric.

"The work of a wizard?" said Tulvgir, his hand falling from his beard, his attention drawn away from the riddle in the stone.

Nodding, Halsedric answered, "Perhaps. A ward without to punish those trying to enter. A ward within to keep what lays within trapped in the stone."

"How does one lay a ward without and within, without remaining in the tomb?"

All eyes turned to the breech. Without saying a word, Tulvgir made his way to the doorway, stepping over the stone that littered the base of the wall. The light of his lamp pierced the dark, rending the thick shadow that hung heavy in that stony domain.

What lay beyond was a chamber, some forty feet square on all sides, the floor bare at the center. Along the sides, however, lay the bones and the scattered remains of those who dared venture in. Corroded tools used to break stone, bits of cloth and leather in various stages of ruin and decay. Portions of cloaks and blankets, knapsacks, and bags. A broken shaft of what might have been from a spear, half a skull overturned on its side amongst other things. It was a grim scene, filled with foreboding. A warning to the brave or the foolhardy, that this place was where death had made its abode.

At the back of the room, slightly offset from where they stood, a hallway ventured further into darkness. "I do not like this place," said Tulvgir barely above his breath.

"All the more reason to be done with our task, and with haste," said Halsedric.

Stepping away from the gap, Tulvgir retrieved his weapon, "Perhaps if you draw your sword. A little more light might be helpful."

"The holy flame that burns in the steel may not burn my flesh, but it will burn all others. If I must take up the sword, it will be only in time of need."

Slowly, they squeezed past the rough portal into the space beyond. At once, a chill fell upon them. Not the biting cold of a winter's day, nor the bracing feel of a deep autumnal wind. This was a grasping sort of chill, damp and penetrating. It wound up from the floor, pressed past clothes like the fingers of the dead, cutting deep into flesh. Tulvgir and Herodiani were the most acutely affected, each of them shivering as they passed from the outside into the interior.

"Do you feel that?" said Tulvgir.

"Yes," Halsedric answered.

As the lamp scanned the interior, they found a curious sight. At the corners of the exterior wall, they found a pile of bones pressed into the crease. Atop them, like the glistening scales of some impossible creature from the sea, lay a shirt of armor that once covered the chest and legs of the deceased. As they neared, the colors changed from silver to blue to violet with hues of yellow and orange. Among the remains rested greaves and a pointed helm of the same strange material.

Tulvgir was the first to approach, kneeling and clearing a space amongst the rubble and debris to set his lamp. His hand moved slowly to the coat of scales, his thick fingers caressing the scales of the mail, withdrawing them suddenly as if with a jolt.

"In all of the wares of my kin, I have never seen such work. What could it be?"

Halsedric followed the example of the Wodeman. Setting his pack against the wall, he found a space next to the bones that lay there and cleared an area where he could kneel. He reached out and touched the mail, felt the fine work like a child first learning his senses. He reached over the mail, taking up the skull that lay near the helm. Lifting it from the ground, Halsedric pushed back the gray frail hairs that once hung free. With both hands he held the skull, his eyes closing, communing with something beyond the understanding of the others.

Eyes snapping open, Halsedric spoke, monotone, as if his mind were far away. "His name was Erloguiandi. One of the Host of the West, come here during the first war. It was he, and his comrade Aeolsareal, who set the wards and remained herein when the tomb was sealed."

Holding back the skull, and looking down with reverence, he continued, "A noble sacrifice. Not chosen, but done willingly. It was he who slew the evil contained within and it was he who remained to ensure that it was locked away for all time."

Inhaling deeply, his head bowed as he slowly exhaled. His silence persisted for a long time, as if in silent prayer.

"Halsedric?" Tulvgir said, breaking the dreadful quiet.

Halsedric was slow to answer. "Let us collect the bones of these fallen heroes and take them away from this terrible place. I will bury them in ground less forsaken, that the spirits they once held may find some peace."

Both Tulvgir and Herodiani went about unloading their gear near that of Halsedric. Untying flaps, they gathered blankets by which they could collect the bones, or as many as they could find. As they did, Halsedric held the skull of Erloguiandi and mouthed a silent prayer for the fallen, whose time in this dark place had been years uncounted and forgotten. Only when he was done did Herodiani gently take up the object and place it with the rest of the remains.

Even as they bundled the cloth that contained the bones, Halsedric turned on his knee. The reverence and sorrow that once graced his face turned hard and defiant as his eyes set their focus deep into the dark of the tunnel that led further into the accursed stone of this dreadful crypt.

Absorbed by his thoughts, he pondered to himself a question that, up to that moment, he hadn't asked before. He had known evil before and wrestled with it. He had smelled the stink of its breath and felt the corruption of its flesh. Yet, how vile could something be that a heavenly creature would offer so great a sacrifice? So as to guarantee that such evil should never be unloosed on the world again?

The only way to know was to venture further.

CHAPTER 10

Their burdens unloaded at the entrance, they pushed into the encumbering black of the tunnel. The light from the lamp cut deep swaths into the curtain of dark that hung like a suffocating tapestry before them. From the entrance, the upper level of the tomb consisted of two rectangular chambers connected by a hallway. Walls were cut straight and equal being roughly twelve feet high, with a hallway wide enough that three could walk abreast. For a hundred paces the way was straight and level until it opened into the chamber at the other end. There awaited a stairway that spiraled down and around a cylindrical shaft bored out of the stone, the steps carved straight from the encircling wall. The pit itself plunged down into the earth for two stories or more.

It wasn't just the creeping cold that clawed at them or the uncanny stillness that covered them like a blanket. Even as Tulvgir peered down into the hole in which the stair wound, he couldn't help but comment.

"Many a dark place I have been, and many a silent cavern I have trod. I am master of obsidian, opal, and granite. Yet, of all the places I have gone, this place sets a warning to my heart. As if the ghosts of the damned live within the very rock itself."

Echoes of a raven barking outside the tomb mocked them in the black as they made their descent, a sound ominous enough to give them all pause. Under her breath, Herodiani said something in her native tongue, a short and beautiful strain of words that almost made the curse she uttered sound pleasant.

Halsedric heard this, and one corner of his mouth curled up amused, remembering her errant shot at the raven. Of all the years he had known her, he had never seen her miss. Even an expert is off sometimes. But for her, a near miss was as much as being off by a mile. He knew the blunder—whether of her own volition or of some dark spell cast by unseen hands—grated at her from within. While she never engaged in any activity where she might lose, when involved, however, she never lost. Whether it be skill with a bow, skill with a blade, gamesmanship, or the hunt.

The call of the bird was soon followed by the soft scuffle of feet on stone and punctuated by the hard hollow thump of Tulvgir's boots. Step upon step, their trek spiraled around the circumference of the hole, the lamplight cutting the darkness like a lighthouse beacon. The illuminating shaft turned this way and that, at first reflecting off drab mountain stone and then bouncing away.

Herodiani sniffed the air and grumbled softly. Soon, Halsedric did the same, noting something foul.

"What is that stench?" remarked Tulvgir half-heartedly, preoccupied with following the light and what it revealed.

"Death, I think," answered Halsedric.

"Down here?" said Herodiani.

Crypts were not new to Halsedric. They could be dusty, dank, and almost always cold. Moldering smells were commonplace in such environs, the aftereffects of long decay. This odor, however, was too new for a tomb as old as this. As they reached the bottom of the stair, Halsedric paused.

"Stay back," he warned.

Hand firmly on hilt, he drew his sword. The blade hummed and screeched as a creeping red glow moved from hilt to tip, colorful flames consuming the steel with all the subtlety of a match to gasoline. At once, the area around them was illuminated, the shadows that once clung to them now relegated to corners, niches, and depressions where the light could not reach.

The other two instinctively backed up a half-step, still wary of the holy fire. While there was surety in the avenging light, there too was also danger. A gift from the Creator, the justice it wrought was a tool of good. Fire, however, was still fire, untamed and unbridled until quenched.

"Evil is here," said Herodiani, her hands tensing on her bow.

"It is in the very mountainside," added Tulvgir.

"Let us hope that is all it is," said Halsedric.

As they pressed forward, the stench only grew stronger. They went another hundred paces or so before the combined light found the opening ahead. Tulvgir coughed reactively as they pressed into the chamber before them, Herodiani turning her head away from the retching odor as if that would make any difference. Here, the odor was the strongest, with even Halsedric wrinkling his nose at the smell.

Within they found a morbid, if not puzzling, sight. The chamber itself was rectangular in shape some fifty feet wide and thirty feet deep. The stone of the ceiling went up at angles, creating a vault of sorts nearly the height of three tall men, if not more. At the far end, barely visible from where they stood, were three open portals spaced at even intervals. These were just high enough for a man to enter without stooping, and as wide as a man and a half. In the middle of the chamber, a crude altar was raised. The base of it was made of stacked stone, some with rounded parts— the remnants of a much larger stone crafted into a great disk. Others were rudely fashioned from granite blocks. On top of this makeshift pedestal a flat slab was laid, an oblong rectangle several hands longer than that of a man. The edges were rough, uncouthly cut from a much larger piece. Bones littered the ground here, some human, some not. A pile of remains rested along the left wall, discarded there purposely. Stains brown, red, and black covered the altar as well as the ground around it, testifying to the grim use for which it was erected. This was a place of sacrifice, much like the statues that guarded this dread realm.

Herodiani recoiled at the sight, and Tulvgir turned his eyes away, saying nothing. After a time, Herodiani asked, "The work of the cult?"

"The Four?" said Halsedric, lifting his sword up higher, and letting the light of the many-colored flames paint the interior. "I think not. This is something else, I fear."

The trio moved cautiously inside, each of them scanning the room and whatever details the lights uncovered. The beam from the lamp seemed to dance of its own accord, reflecting off the walls, revealing writing sloppily scribed in an unknown tongue.

As Halsedric approached the script, he scanned the lettering. Each rune drawn looked as if it were traced by an angry and spiteful hand. The drips from the varied letters were pulled down by gravity, unintentionally connecting lines above and below before they hardened and dried. The longer he spied the walls, the more of the writing was revealed, none of it looking as if it was done with paint or ink.

"What is this?" asked the Wodeman.

Halsedric drew near, looking down the length of the chamber, sword raised high. The whole of the wall was completely covered by the script and symbols, the others painted accordingly. For a time, he stared blankly, wondering. "It is no tongue of which I am familiar. Older, I think."

"Do I dare ask with what ink they used?"

"You need not ask the question if you already know the answer, my friend. Blood, I think. Mixed with a binder."

In unison, they gathered at the altar, inspecting it closer. By now, they became accustomed to the smell, though it was as thick as soup within this place. Near the top, along what was left of the original arc, writing cut into the stone. This script, however, unlike that upon the walls, appeared more like the lettering that Halsedric bore on his chest. Various stains covered the face, the whole of the rock covered in gore long dried hard.

Lifting up his sword, Halsedric looked toward the back of the chamber. "Tulvgir, cast the light of your lamp to the back wall," he commanded in a soft voice.

As Herodiani moved to the opposite end of the altar, Tulvgir shone the lamp along the length of the back wall.

Here they found the three openings, each opening up to a smaller chamber beyond, the details of which the lamp could not fully unveil.

Looking down at the altar, Halsedric pointed with his hand at the script cut into the stone of the altar. "These are the capstones to the tombs, I think. The wards have been breached, and the tombs open."

"Then it is true," said Herodiani. "He has been loosed."

"Then we should leave this foul place and report what we have found," Tulvgir said as the light from his lamp fell. "Leave this place as naught but an ill memory. The sooner the better I say."

"The vaults may still be sealed," Halsedric answered.

Small bones and fragments of chipped and broken stone skidded and clacked along the stone floor as Halsedric edged his way forward.

Tulvgir grumbled his discontent. "If the wards of the capstones have been broken, so too will the wards on the vault. Best we leave now before something else here is disturbed."

Turning slightly to face Tulvgir, Halsedric replied, "Stay here, my friend, if your courage fails you." Slowly, his gaze returned to that of the back of the chamber, his sword aloft. "This was my mission, not yours."

Thick fingers loosened and gripped once more the handle of his mace, tighter now than before. A low rumble in his throat and a pinched face followed a sidelong look at Halsedric as Tulvgir muttered, "No need for insults."

Sniffing in jest, Halsedric paused to revel in the humor of the moment. "Herodiani, take the stair up and keep watch on the entrance."

Halsedric continued toward the back, eyes alternating between the back wall and the floor below. Each step he took with purpose, slowly moving away the debris on the ground with his toe or the side of his boot before going forward.

Tulvgir followed behind treading the same path, his light scanning the walls at times, revealing more of the hard harsh lettering that covered them. "The runes are everywhere," he noted.

Halsedric said nothing, his attention fixed on the first crypt to the right. He stopped at the doorway, commanding Tulvgir to shed the light of his lamp at the floor of the entrance. Cut into the stone of the floor was a wide circular trench fitted for a circular capstone, chipped at the edges where it was rolled away or pulled down. They went about looking at the outer walls, where large chunks of stone were pulled away, the pattern of the destruction being dotted in a circular form.

"It looks as if whatever sealed this tomb was torn away, and the stone with it," said Tulvgir in a hushed voice.

As the beam broke the dark of the chamber's interior, a different scene revealed itself much to their horror.

The chamber that held the vault was narrow, just wide and long enough to contain a pedestal of stone. Upon this a leaden vault rested. The dull gray sheen of the metal was now blacked and corroded at the ribs. The upturned lid resting against the back wall was enough to tell them what they already suspected. Whatever was within was now freed. Whatever bonds were used, whatever magic kept the contents within restrained, were nullified. But that was not all the light revealed.

There, on the space around the base of the pedestal, lay a heap of bodies, some naked, some clothed, though what garbed them was little more than rags. The stench they gave off was intense and horrible, causing both Halsedric and Tulvgir to lift a hand to their noses and turn away with unwanted gasps.

Recovered now, Halsedric dared a closer look. Some had hair that remained on their scalps, though thready and thin. Others were bald. The once pink skin of the living had turned a milky gray-white. The corpses were heaped in a chaotic array, some showing the maroon-colored scars of rent flesh, perhaps from battle, perhaps from something else. Yet there was something about them that made Halsedric look closer, something that seemed out of place. It took him a moment or two of study as Tulvgir cleared his throat impatiently.

"Quiet," answered Halsedric in whispered tones as he returned to his inspection. Kneeling, he held the light of his sword closer to a leg that stuck out from the mass of dead flesh. Long he looked before standing up and turning slightly.

"The blood," Halsedric said, looking down at Tulvgir.

Tulvgir returned the remark with puzzled eyes. He squinted briefly, a wordless question that Halsedric was quick to reply.

"The blood. It pools at the lowest point when a body dies." Halsedric faced the crypt again, scanning the pale bodies that cluttered the narrow sparse space. None of them showed the familiar splotches and bruising indicative of blood that had pooled and settled. Not even those at the bottom.

Halsedric's eyes caught the dull yellow feature of a long nail, something that one might find on the end of an eagle's talon, save much longer. It stuck out from the tangled mesh of limbs and bodies. He spied a foot where the toes were melted together, a long cleft forming in the flesh down the middle.

Using his left hand, Halsedric pulled a dagger from his belt. A narrow blade whose tip was wicked sharp, he held the blade out, close to one of the exposed limbs of the pale mass. Taking an anxious breath or two, he turned slightly back to Tulvgir. "Be prepared to run," he whispered.

Slowly the dagger moved forward until the tip of it pressed against the milky-gray flesh of an exposed calf. Pressing past the skin, Halsedric drew the tip down, not more than an inch, before pulling it free. A dark sort of gel oozed out from the cut, thicker than blood, being more black than red. In the still moments that passed, Halsedric watched the mass of appendages and tangled flesh, his nervous eyes seeking movement or sound. None was seen.

Breathing a relieved sigh, Halsedric rose, wiping the tip of his blade on his sleeve before returning the dagger to its holder. He waited for a time, expecting a reaction but quietly praying he had not invited peril. Nothing moved in that cold dead place. Whatever these creatures were, they remained inanimate, whatever life that once stirred them to action having expired.

Halsedric breathed deep again, pulling back from the crypt. "Let us check the others."

Slowly, the two warriors moved from the one crypt to inspect the others in the same fashion. One by one they uncovered the same scene—the lid of the vault over-turned, its interior empty and a tangled pile of bodies crowding the space in the gaps. Despite what he saw, Halsedric dared to ponder the thought that maybe Tulvgir was right. Perhaps they should have left well enough alone and fled this place when they could.

CHAPTER 11

Having vanished in the thick gloom that surrounded them, Herodiani departed for the entrance, scouting the way back. Tulvgir and Halsedric paused at the exit of the chamber where the three crypts were located. Their attention was drawn to the runes that covered the smooth gray walls. Soon enough, the light from the lamp began to dim.

The tines of Tulvgir's mace made a soft plinking sound against the stony floor as the Wodeman set the weapon aside. Kneeling on the cold stone floor he went about recharging the stones that gave his lamp light. A hollow scrape of brass against brass sounded after the latch on the lamp was lifted, the stones rumbling in their gilded cage before tumbling out onto his wide meaty hand.

The sound seemed greater here. Grander. Every footfall resounded in the dreadful silence, where outside only the most sensitive ears might have heard their approach. It was unnerving in a way, as if down in the depths of the mountain stone the empty halls were too silent, too lifeless.

The crack of the light-stones sounded like a shot being fired, piercing Halsedric's ears. His brow furrowed briefly in disdain, looking down, then up again, thinking twice about the complaint he was going to raise. Lifting the sword, the vivid flames along the keen edges bending and swaying like dancers on a deadly line. He scanned the writing on the walls, alternately repelled and fascinated by it.

"This script is old, I think," he said in a hushed tone.

"How old?" The question was a half-hearted one, mindlessly said by Tulvgir as he worked to get the lamp into working order.

Halsedric squinted, partly because of the light that bounced and writhed off of the wall as Tulvgir rolled the light stones back into his lamp. The gears in his head were turning. The lettering looked familiar. He whispered a name, "Wurn."

A latch closed on the lamp with a muted click. "What say you?" asked Tulvgir.

"Wurn." Halsedric said the name with purpose now. "A scribe I knew many years past. He would know what these runes mean and from what vile race they spring."

"Cathars?"

"They use pictures as words," answered Halsedric. "The Hakan use a script very much like that of your kin." He paused for a moment, considering his words. "This flows. Like blood from a wound or the writhing of an angry viper. I have seen such from scrolls that were borne out of the Far East, where it is said a sea of sand resides. Similar, but not."

Metal tines scraped discordantly against stone as Tulvgir rose to his feet, the handle of his mace in one hand, the lamp in the other. A harsh sound pierced the dead space, with Halsedric first thinking it a curse from a harsh tongue. Instinctively, he turned his head sideways, his ears aching to hear some unnatural sound to follow.

Tulvgir started to speak, only to be hushed by Halsedric, his ears straining to listen in the silence.

"Did you hear?" Halsedric whispered.

Head tilted sideways, eyes looking at his companion out of their corners, Tulvgir made a quizzical grunt. Then, more silence.

Halsedric inhaled deeply, the look of concern heavy on his brow. "Nothing," he said quietly.

With a measure of reluctance in his eyes, Halsedric turned his attention to his sword. "We have no more need of this now," he said as he deftly returned the weapon back to its sheath. The orange-hot flaming brand was soundlessly quenched as it slid into the scabbard by his side. The world around them darkened as the fire of his blade was extinguished, as if the cold specter of evil somehow crept back into the room.

"I rather wish you had kept it at the ready," Tulvgir grumbled. "It gave comfort in this lifeless place."

Halsedric lifted one side of his mouth in a pleased sort of grin. "You mean to tell me, old friend, you have come to fear the dark deeps of the earth?"

Snorting defiantly, the eyes of Tulvgir squinted and his face twisted. "Of course not," he protested. His annoyance at the jab faded quickly as his countenance softened. Eyes turning this way and that, he checked the shadows in the periphery. Nervously he whispered, "I have delved deeper places than this, and braved the darkness of the unknown. Yet, of all the places I have been, none have given my heart as much desire to see the sunlight again as this wretched place. We have uncovered what we have sought to uncover. It is best that we not linger here, heedless of the warnings of our guide."

"You are correct. Let us not tarry here."

Exiting from the chamber, they moved toward the spiral stair, their footfalls light so as to not disturb that which they could not see, a cone of light from the lamp guiding them. Yet, they had not even gone fifty paces before Halsedric stopped. His head twitched slightly, his brows downturned in sober contemplation.

Tulvgir had gone only a few paces more before he too stopped. Realizing the absence of sound in his haste to leave, he sensed the missing footfalls of his companion.

When the cone of the lamp found him, Halsedric was standing erect and alert, his head turning slightly to his right.

Slowly, Tulvgir approached, closing the gap. "Why do you—"

Tulvgir went mute as Halsedric's hand shot up in warning. As the echoes died away, they both listened in silence, ears reaching out to hear even the slightest sound. As his head craned more, the rustle of his clothes was like the heralding winds of a storm in the dead still of the hallway. When that died away, all returned to the crushing quiet that saturated the tomb.

Long, anxious moments passed, with nothing coming to ear save the near imperceptible whistle of breath entering and exiting their nostrils. Nothing stirred in the stony tomb. Not the squeak of a rat, nor the pitter patter of its tiny feet; not the clicking of a spider's legs, nor the twang of the strands of its web.

Halsedric's eyes expressed confusion and trouble and a flush came over his face like the blush of a newly-wedded bride.

"What?" said Tulvgir.

Halsedric blinked into the light, his eyes focused into a thousand-mile stare. The query hung in the air like the ill stench that still surrounded them, waiting for a clean breeze to blow it away. Several seconds passed, though they felt like an eternity.

"Did you feel that?" asked Halsedric.

"What say you?"

Another long and soul-sickening pause. Halsedric's head twisted around again, and this time his body followed.

In fear, Tulvgir held his breath, expecting something to scream out from the gloom that persisted behind them. His lamp strayed onto the doorway from which they came, part of it blocked by the frame of Halsedric. There it stayed, reflecting off the gray dull stone of the root of the mountain where they now stood.

Halsedric, for his part, listened and waited. His eyes closed, and the search of his ears reached out into the still, dense air that filled the hallway, hoping to hear something. A chill ran through his spine. Starting at the base of his neck and filling his shoulders, it rushed down his back like a river of tiny pinpricks along his skin. It was a sensation not unfamiliar to him—he had felt it before. Long ago. His mind raced to remember when and where, clawing through memories of the long years.

Slowly, Halsedric turned back to face his friend, his gaze meeting the puzzled eyes of the Wodeman.

"What spell has taken you?" said Tulvgir.

Slow to answer, his eyes fell even as his hands tightened around the grip of his hilt. In time, his eyes lifted, and he answered his friend. "I felt something. Malevolent. An ill memory of a time and a place long past. Ancient. Hidden. And yet…"

Halsedric's attention returned to the room they just left. He paused for a moment, searching both senses and recollections.

"What?"

With a blank stare, Halsedric answered, "I know naught."

"The Lord of Bones?"

After a time, Halsedric shook his head. "Let us be gone from this place."

They continued their trek toward the stair, though their pace this time was quicker. Twenty paces, then thirty, the sound of footfalls keeping time and count of their departure. At the foot of the spiral stair, Halsedric felt it again. The same sensation as before. Here he stopped and turned in full, looking behind them, his eyes doing their best to pierce the veil of murky black.

This time, Tulvgir was less hasty and more alert. Two stairs up he stopped and turned back, the light of the lamp showing on Halsedric again. His lamp pressed into the dark, illuminating anything the shadows might be hiding.

It wasn't a sign of movement that Halsedric sought in that dread place, it was sound. The recollection of a foreboding wail from the depths of a cave. A sound that shook him to his marrow. The memory of that moment came back in a rush. In it, his legs were weak and a warm rush of blood overtook his abdomen. Crimson rivulets whose fingers traced themselves down his thigh, staining cloth and skin. The only sound that drowned out the last gurgling gasps of the woman he slew. The horrible decision he made, ceding the honor he held dear for the command of the God that made him. An end to the horrors he had seen and to the evil he contested. It was that sound his ears itched to hear. An ill remembrance buried in the deep soil that is the forgetfulness of long years.

He was answered with silence. Dead silence. A secret hope and dread that never came. Was it just him? Was it nothing more than the resurfacing of a time he had longed to forget?

Halsedric had long made peace with his fate. He had come to accept what he was and who he was now, even as hard as it was to believe in the beginning. The words of the Prophet Jalamil were always there, retained like a precious gem, one too beautiful to sell or trade.

Returning to the moment, Halsedric inhaled deeply, releasing a breath long and furtive. Turning back, he wordlessly motioned Tulvgir to ascend. If there was something still down there, be it ghost or flesh-bound, now was not the time to contest it. Urgency dictated haste. To report their findings, and let wiser minds determine the next course of action.

His sword rattled in its scabbard, the gilded iron of his hilt banging against brass with each upward step. Head down, Halsedric kept his eyes on the stone stair, lest the darkness deceive him. One misplaced step meant a stony reception for a hard fall. There was peace in the monotony. The rhythmic thump of Tulvgir's boots, followed by the soft shuffle of his, stair after stair. Halfway up, however, something changed. The light of the lamp moved away, and the steady pace of Tulvgir no longer matched his own. He came to this realization only a half-moment before running into the Wodeman in front of him. Coming to a sudden halt, he nearly lost his footing as gravity pulled him back. Righting himself, Halsedric lifted his head.

What he saw gave him a moment of pause, partly out of confusion but also of surprise. Tulvgir held the lamp, but the light pointed further up, at least five stairs above them. Looking past the Wodeman and following the light, he saw the familiar shape of Herodiani crouched there on the steps. Her moss-colored cloak almost covered her in full, the hood pulled back. A portion of her bow stuck out from the gap, the hint of an arrow head along with it. Her piercing blue eyes shone bright in the lamp's lemon glow, their gaze fixed directly on Halsedric.

As he went to inquire, Herodiani lifted her free hand, a finger pressed to her lips, bidding silence.

CHAPTER 12

"Something awaits us outside the tomb," whispered Herodiani.

Even after a whisper, the emptiness of the lifeless halls made her words sound like a sudden rush of wind through the leaves.

"What is it?" asked Halsedric.

"You shall see."

Halsedric and the Wodeman followed after the Elanni huntress, moving in stealth to the entrance. As they approached the exit, Tulvgir laid his lamp with their gear, piled in the tomb near the entrance. While the others crouched toward the ledge, the Wodeman remained in the dark spaces of the cleft. Two was more than enough to spy what awaited them below.

With Herodiani kneeling in front of him, Halsedric's head inched its way up from a crouching position, eyes seeking activity among the mounds below. With her Elanni cloak surrounding her, the huntress was able to all but vanish into the shadows of the cleft in the mountainside. Barely hidden beneath her cloak was her bow, a white-fletched arrow ready in the bow string.

"Do you see him?" she whispered.

Most of the detail of the forms that milled about below was blocked from Halsedric's vantage point. They appeared to be men of some sort. One had a nest of hair that reminded him of dense brambles, naked at the shoulders. Another wore a helmet that looked caked with rust, the top of it coming to a conical point. A third wore mail and a bucket helm covering its face in full, the metal of it thick with a ruddy patina. The shirt of rings it wore looked tattered and torn, as if it were more rags than mail. Past it jutted out the point of the sword it carried.

The most striking part of the scene, however, was a dark figure lying against the curve of one of the mounds. Clothed hood to toe in black, it wore a cape that had a peculiar sheen to it and a fringe uneven in appearance. Even from the distance, it reminded Halsedric of the tail feathers of a bird. With hood entirely up and head pressed sideways against the loose pile of broken stones, the figure chanted in an eldritch tongue, the words confused and clouded by an occasional whistle of wind.

"Black," mumbled Halsedric, noting the color of the figure's clothes.

"Like the down of a crow," added Herodiani.

"Like the down of a raven," Halsedric corrected.

A stillness grew between them as Halsedric observed the goings on below, breaking the silence only when he said, "I knew I had an ill feeling about that accursed bird."

"I counted five, all told," said Herodiani. "Including the dark conjurer."

Lowering himself and backing away, Halsedric added, "It will be six, soon enough if that chant continues."

Tulvgir waited further back in the fissure, Halsedric backing up slowly to avoid running into the Wodeman.

Herodiani pulled back from her crouch, letting the shadows of the mountain passage obscure her as she withdrew from the overlook.

"Six is no match for us," Tulvgir said, one hand on the handle of his mace, another on the shaft closer to the head. He nervously spun the weapon along its shaft, eager for a scrap.

"It is not the fight I fear, but the dark conjurer below," replied Halsedric in a low voice. "He was able to evade a deadly dart once."

"With magic, no doubt," grumbled Herodiani softly.

"I have no desire for him to evade us again," continued Halsedric.

"He is prone now, and occupied," said Herodiani. "A well-placed dart and it will be the end of him."

"Agreed," answered Halsedric with a nod. Turning on his heel, he addressed Tulvgir.

"Stay near her," he pointed to the huntress, "and make ready to defend her should things go awry." Pausing, he looked at the broken entrance of the tomb. For a long second, his eyes fixed on the gloom that lay beyond. "I will collect our things."

The soles of his feet hissed and whispered as he quickly rotated back to Herodiani. "Wait until my call before doing the deed. Make your aim true…and deadly. No second chances with this one."

Her eyes narrowed as Herodiani reacted to the last few words. As plainly delivered as it was, it was nonetheless received as a rebuke.

As much as Halsedric understood this, he had little care for the words he spoke or the meaning others found in them. Once more, his focus returned to the entrance of the tomb. A brief moment of distraction hit him as he stood there, occupied with his thoughts, of what it was he saw in that lifeless place. Something that pricked at him, an itch he could not scratch.

"Is that all?" said Herodiani.

Eyes fixed in a distracted gaze and speaking with a voice that sounded a thousand miles away, Halsedric answered, "Make ready and wait for my command." He made his way to the broken threshold of the tomb, leaving the others.

Hands on both sides of the wall, Halsedric dipped his head back into the black, scanning the room to locate their packs and the bones they collected. His eye caught the glint of the armor the old guardians wore, illuminated partly by the lamp of Tulvgir. It was as if the stray light sought the items out, preferring the scales of the mail to the challenge of the dark. Slowly he shuffled in, turned, and made his way to the corner where one of the guardians once laid. Kneeling, he cradled the helm the ancient warrior wore until his dying breath. As helms went, it looked larger than that of those he had seen before, and lighter. Yet, his mind puzzled after the sheen of the metal and the mystery of it. He was holding something crafted in the forges of a heavenly realm beyond. An object conceived by the will of something holy, fashioned by hands infinitely more skilled than the most cunning craftsmen of the Elanni or the Wodemen. Not a single dent or blemish marred the exterior. Turning the helm this way and that, he further pondered the mystery of it with a measure of awe. Strange in its nature, it was still yet familiar in a way that he could not totally fathom.

More puzzled by the artifact than before, he laid the thing back down on the ground with reverence.

It was while Halsedric was gathering their gear at the entrance that something caught his attention. His head turned with a snap, his eyes pierced the pitch black of the greater tomb. This time, it wasn't a vague feeling or some strange remembrance from his past. It was a soft sound, almost inaudible. A whisper? A sigh? The soft shuffle of feet? The ragged echo of it hid its true nature.

For a time, Halsedric stood there, stock still. His eyes closed, ears open to any and every sound. It wasn't the noise he heard that troubled him, but the feeling in his gut. The very same feeling he had down on the lower level and the grim reminiscing of an encounter still yet unresolved. The hair on the back of his neck felt stiff as the unwelcome tingle in his gut remained.

Hastily, he returned to the entrance. One by one he grabbed their things, relocating them to the fissure in the mountainside before deciding he needed to investigate further. Looking up, he saw the pair at the entrance of the cleft. Herodiani was kneeling, bow at the ready. Covered head to toe in her Elanni cloak, her form was obscured, making her almost part of the shadows. Tulvgir, however, knelt behind her, his mighty mace in his hand, the thick, heavy sole of one boot facing him.

The Wodeman twisted about, shuffling on his knees, looking back at Halsedric with expectation. As Halsedric laid the bones down against the cleft of the wall, he raised his head and his eyes met the expectant gaze of Tulvgir.

With a wordless understanding, Halsedric raised a single finger, his eyes saying more than his hands. Wait until the signal is given.

With a single nod, Tulvgir signaled his understanding.

Entering back into the tomb once more, Halsedric grabbed the lamp with his left hand and pointed it at the hallway that led to the crypts. For a time, he stood there in silence, wondering if, as before, something waited just beyond the light of the lamp.

With slow and purposeful steps, Halsedric moved further into the tomb, retracing steps he had trod earlier. Twenty paces into the hallway, Halsedric's right hand went to the hilt of his sword. The further he ventured into the dark, the more the sickness in his gut grew. It wasn't a stray sound now. It was a feeling, tangible and real. With each step forward, the gathering doom grew.

Fifty steps now, and the beam of the light traced the hazy outline of the circular hole and the stairway down. His senses tingled, his ears buzzing, his eyes looking for even the most minute movement in the grainy shadows. He didn't have to guess now or wonder. Something was there in the dark. A whisper floated up, or was it a shuffle? Instinctively, he paused. Bending down, he set down the lamp before throwing back his cloak. Fingers gripping the hilt tightly, he pulled his sword with purpose. As before, the blade glowed an orange-cherry red before bursting into colored flames with a pop. At once, the hallway saw the life of light as shadows gave way. Sword at the fore, he bent down once again and took the lamp by its handle. Edging his way forward, the rim of the stairway down neared, the features of it becoming clearer. At the top he stopped and pointed the lamp downward while holding the sword up high.

In the dread and drear of the pit below, a grave sight came to his worried eyes. Pale shapes in the dark moved somewhere below. The glow of his sword was just enough to catch the movements in the blanket of black. When the lamp was raised, however, it revealed a sight more terrible than he imagined. Pale-skinned figures ascended the spiral stair, one or two abreast, coiling upwards like a snake from the pits. Some moved on all fours, others half crouched. These things he knew because he had seen them only minutes before, piled around the stone pedestals of each crypt. Bleached, colorless, lifeless, bloodless, moving under the direction of a will that transcended the grave. Where the tangle of flesh and limbs obscured the finer details, the light of the lamp now revealed. In the brief, horrifying moments his eyes scanned the oncoming mob, Halsedric saw forms that were once men but now had become something else. Varying in states of transition, some retained their failing humanity, save for the pale, milky skin. Their modesty was maintained with rags, wearing the last shreds of clothing they owned or ever would own. A few still sported the head of hair they once had in life, though others displayed gradual states of loss. Others showed to what end their transition would take. Vaguely human in form, their finer details were altered, giving them an alien appearance. Five fingers melded and merged into three, each tipped with a yellow talon. The toes of their feet elongated into two digits, cleft at the center, and each adorned with a nail in the manner of their fingers. Utterly bereft of hair from head to toe, their heads looked swollen at the crown and distended at the back.

As the light caught them, a few of the creatures looked up startled. Eyes that were once white and adorned with colored irises were obliterated by a wash of glistening black. A collective hiss rose from the pit as the light struck them. Open mouths revealed an array of fangs—white, triangular, curved and elongated like an interlocking set of tiny slicing ivory shards.

As horrified as he was, Halsedric stood his ground at the top, his sword held high. Stunned at first, the approaching fiends initially recoiled at the sight of the revenant and his blade. Hissing quickly changed, a ratcheting, stuttering growl taking its place. Halted in their place for the moment, some lunged, threatening to attack, the façade of their bravado restrained by an inner fear. Like a snake of many parts, the line of creatures tensed, twitched, threatened, but hesitated by what it perceived to be a superior foe.

His sword hand dropped and Halsedric shifted his feet, expecting a fight. Even as the mass below him quavered indecisive, it was more than clear that sheer numbers were on their side. His eyes followed the rim of the stone void from whence the stair emerged. Graven-faced, he knew it was only a matter of time before fear wasn't enough to restrain the oncoming host. Every predator tests it prey, and this was no exception. In his mind's eye, he saw them push forward, perhaps sacrificing a few to his blade while others scrambled up the wall, outside the reach of his sword. The mass of their numbers would flank and overwhelm him. Silently, he began to pray, his lips moving and the words coming in a tense whisper.

"God of my fathers, give me wisdom. Give me strength."

The creatures inched forward, slavering jaws and snapping teeth greeting him. One broke forward, rushing at him in a frenzied haste. The flames of Halsedric's sword roared as the weapon cut the air. When the stroke fell, the forward part of the blade cut deep the ivory flesh, cleaving the creature from shoulder to chest in a single stroke. The ripped flesh sizzled like oil in a hot pan as the blessed blade rent corrupted flesh and bone. As the fiend fell back, it collided with one of its fellows, both tumbling into the pit below.

A second creature ascended, breaking from the others. This one found itself impaled through the face, Halsedric thrusting his blade forward at an opportune time. Boot raised, he kicked the dying creature from his blade, the light stones rattling in their cage of brass.

"Back to the abyss with you, foul beasts!" Halsedric's voice boomed in the stony halls, the gold lettering on his chest seeming to glow in the light of his blade. The rebuke sounded feeble on its face—a pointless course of action as one man stood against a wave of enemies. Yet, something about the words stilled the hissing and growling of the pale fiends. For a moment, it seemed that sheer faith and will was enough to keep them at bay.

It was not to last. One head turned, and then another, as probing eyes started to scan the rim of the stair above them, a plan beginning to take shape in the collective, controlling will that drove these beasts forward.

His position about to be compromised, Halsedric slowly started to withdraw. There was only one way to stem this tide of darkness, he reasoned. With that, he made a mad dash in the darkness to the narrow door where the others waited.

CHAPTER 13

"Loose the arrow," came the cry from the tomb. Halsedric's words traveled with the echoes, soft at first, but clear enough for Herodiani to hear. Her eyes had never left her target, the figure in the cloak of black feathers as it lay on the mound of broken stone. The chanting stopped and the hooded head lifted in alarm.

"Take him," muttered Tulvgir, his voice thick with urgency.

Her actions were quick and purposeful. Arrow readied in the string of the bow, she lifted herself, balancing on one knee. Looking down the line of the shaft, Herodiani noted her mark. With a grunt, she pulled back hard and sure, the limbs of the bow groaning beneath the strain. With a snap and a twang, the bowstring set the missile flying, the projectile whistling softly as it cut the air. There was no trickery this time, no sudden change of direction or deflection of the arrow's flight. The whistle ended when the arrow struck true, piercing the cloth of the hood and skewering whatever flesh lay beneath. Twitching at first, the mysterious sorcerer spun about, his hands reaching up to the end of the arrow as he fell backward. Stones tumbled from the mound with a rumbling clack, falling over the cloaked figure as it fell to the ground.

Not wasting any time, Herodiani sent a second arrow flying, this time the missile hitting hard just left of center of the sorcerer's chest with a hollow thump—a mortal wound. Whatever was cloaked in those black garments heaved slightly before moving no more.

Two impossible shots for any mortal, Tulvgir knew, but not for Herodiani. He rose straight up behind her, his mace held at the ready in both hands. "Leave the remainder to me," he said to her in a bold and haughty tone as he stepped around her. He headed directly to the top of the exterior stair. "Halsedric is in need of your aid, I think."

As Herodiani drew away, Tulvgir stopped at the top of the tortured stair, set his feet apart, gripped his mace at the bottom of the shaft, and swung it around. Looking down at the scene below, he saw his opponents milling around confused, two of the dead creatures taking the chance to look up from whence the arrows came. With narrow eyes and a satisfied grin, the Wodeman grimly shouted down, "Come up, my friends, come up! I will give you a taste of fine mountain steel. A portion, no doubt, you shall choke on."

***

Halsedric skidded to a stop and turned about in the dark expanse of the chamber. His back to the entrance, he stood only a few paces from the daylight outside. The lamp, aided by the light cast from the holy flame of his blade, revealed the movements of the creatures that pursued. Filing out from the hallway, they grew like an angry swarm, moving at a quick pace at first, but slowing quickly as their prey turned to confront them. Despite the obvious advantage they had over him, there was a reticence to face their foe. Hisses and snarls issued from the mass of pale fiends like dogs snarling at a stranger. Even as their numbers grew at the flanks, the monsters took care to not get too close for fear of the blade and the hand that wielded it.

His head turning with a snap, Halsedric called out to Herodiani once more, the urgency of their predicament dripping from each word. "Down the sorcerer. Take him now!" A frantic call, but needless. Occupied with matters of his own, Halsedric was unaware Herodiani had done the deed.

Eyes forward once more, he sized up the situation, a few of the stooped creatures daring to take a step forward. Sword out front, he waved his flaming weapon menacingly, screaming out a throaty, "Hah!"

The mass of white-skinned creatures leapt back at once, their numbers still not outweighing their caution. Like pack wolves confronting bigger game, they were cagy enough to let reason outweigh whatever hunger drove them. Halsedric withdrew a step, and in response, the pack moved forward, barking, snarling, and hissing with an even greater resolve. The stones inside the lamp clanked against the thin brass as he repeated his threat, the flames of his sword roaring as the edge cut the air. The response from the pack was the same, whipping up an even greater hatred of the warrior that defied them.

Head turning sharply to the right, Halsedric went to call out another plea for Herodiani to take her shot. The cry was stifled in his throat as he spied a figure out of the corner of his eye. Reflexively, he crouched and swerved to his left just in time to hear a dart whistling above. True to its aim, it struck one of the creatures in its left eye, the shaft of the arrow embedded deep in its skull. The thing collapsed to the ground, falling like a stuffed doll, rejected by its owner for another plaything. Halsedric rose slowly, his eyes fixed on the demons in the dark. A sudden still fell over that blackened expanse, the shock of the retaliation taking them all unawares. No hissing, no growls or snarls. Just a dreadful, impossible stillness as if Halsedric were standing in the eye of some evil storm.

Standing straight once more, Halsedric took no time to skip back one step, then another, his head turning this way and that as he did. When his back hit solid stone, he slunk through the entrance and into the cleft that led to the tomb.

Here at the hewn entrance, Halsedric knew he could hold them off, the numbers of his pursuers holding little advantage. Holding out the lamp in his left hand, he felt the delicate fingers of Herodiani take the device from him.

"Get the bags and the bones," he commanded to her. "We are leaving this place with haste."

"What of them?"

"The light," answered Halsedric.

"The light?"

"Black eyes work best in dark. The sun still reigns high here. Distance before eventide is our best defense. Now be quick about it."

The point of his sword guarding the doorway, Halsedric stood guard while the sound of shuffling feet and rustling cloth floated to his ears. In the background, the boasts and grim laughter of Tulvgir could be heard as well as the sound of his mace cracking the brittle bones of his latest victim. The lamp now gone, the shadows had reclaimed the interior, the sunset glow of his blade doing little to hold back the heavy gloom. Inside, there was little sound, save the shuffling of flesh against bare rock. Something called to him, deep from within the interior. A whisper of a voice, harsh and malevolent.

"Arargh hag ramashatha."

His skin prickled and the hair once more rose on the back of Halsedric's head as the first beads of sweat formed on his brow. A rush of something struck him, like a wind without bluster, rolling off of him and around him like waves of a stormy sea crashing against a rock. His eyes narrowed and his face fell as he peered deeper into the black of that accursed place. There, far in the back, two dots floating in the air like cinders cast up from the coals of a fire. The point of his sword fell, the fingers of his left hand wrapped around the broken edge of the left doorway as he leaned into the black to get a better view of this new evil that called out to him.

With a start, Halsedric pulled back as something moved in the shadow; a blur of white rushing out of the dark. Big and bulbous, it moved with a startling rapidity. Soon he felt the pain of many fangs piercing the cloth of his sleeve and sinking deep into the flesh of his left arm.

Time stopped as he looked down, seeing a bald head of one of the fiends, its mouth clamped down on his left forearm. It pulled this way and that while it did its best to rip muscle and bone from him. Steam or smoke rose almost at once before it released its bite, the creature screaming as if it had just bit down on hot coals.

Halsedric grunted, his face pinched in a grimace from the pain. At once, he lifted his blade with all his might, his sword pressing through flesh and bone. Blood and spit sputtered from the monster as the holy flame contested with corrupted flesh. Flailing violently, the beast shuttered and twisted with such violence that it threatened to pull the sword from Halsedric's grip. His fingers clenched hard on the hilt as he withdrew his wounded limb from the entrance, away from the steaming maw of the screaming thing. With a flash of motion, his fingers gripped the creature by the throat with all of the anxious fury that one might grasp at the head of a viper, trying not to get bitten. Strangling the screech of the thing with one hand, the other pulled free his blade. With a thrust, he cast the creature back into the dark from whence it came.

***

With a grunt, the heavy boot of Tulvgir clumsily kicked away another of his victims. The head of the thing waved and bobbed, reduced to a pulverized mass of flesh and dark viscera. The force of gravity pulled down the lifeless body as it banged and scraped against the rude stone face that held up the ledge where the Wodeman was making his valiant stand. The third of four scrambled up that twisting stair, the final foe climbing upwards and having a rough time of it. This one was weighed down by armor, or what was once armor. Rusting scales clung to rotting leather like some diseased fish, a great bucket helm covering the creature's head. When it once lived, it might have been a mighty warrior, buried with a great sword, an imposing figure even in death. Now, however, like its animated body, it looked rotten and diseased, falling deep into the clutches of disrepair and threatening to fall apart at any moment.

The first two that came at Tulvgir were garbed in little more than rags, though their bodies fared better. Green-gray skin that sagged, the muscle and sinew seemingly detached beneath. Cloudy eyes, and hair hard and brittle, looking more like a collection of twigs than locks. Faces frozen in a perpetual scowl, the attackers were foreboding and grim to behold and frightening to those far less bold than Tulvgir. One had a rusted timbering axe and managed to cut Tulvgir across his left thigh. He paid for that with one swing of the Wodeman's mace. It slammed into his right temple with such force that both flesh and bone came apart with a spray. Dark spots decorated Tulvgir like some grim trophy of that moment, both harrowing and satisfying to the defender of the top stair.

"Come to me, pretty boy," taunted the Wodeman. "Do not leave me here to wait!" He had only been vaguely aware that Herodiani was active behind him, massing their gear at the stone ledge he defended. Only when he heard the sound of her blade come free from its sheath did he bother to turn his head.

"Grab your things and make ready to leave," she said to him.

One hand came free from his mace, darkened with the remains of the foes previously dispatched. Hand out and arm extended in the direction of the last attacker, Tulvgir protested. "Yet, one remains. Will you deny me this small pleasure?"

At once, an impatient scowl graced the face of the Elanni huntress, displeased with her companion's attitude. With little delay, her bow clutched in her left hand, her sword in her right, she pulled around him and descended the stair with the deftness of a cat traversing a narrow fence, halting near where the last attacker clung to the steps. As the attacker ascended another step, her sword came down upon its head, splitting the rusted helm and cleaving deep into the flesh beneath. She struggled a bit, removing the blade, the head bobbing and twisting lifelessly as she struggled. Finally, she pulled it free and turned back to him with a scowl.

"Now, take your things," she barked back at the Wodeman above her. "We leave with haste."

A deeply disappointed rumble rolled up from deep within the throat of the Wodeman. Muttering something in his native tongue, he turned away to pick up his pack by the strap.

***

Halsedric backed away slowly from the entrance of the tomb, his blade thrust out before him. Fearing a tumble as he backed away in cautious retreat, he risked a brief glimpse of what lay behind. Ten paces or so from the ledge, he spied the form of Tulvgir approaching from behind.

"You left a few for me to slay, I hope," said the Wodeman in his usual way. His shoulder shrugged, reacting to the pull of the pack on one shoulder. "My mace has not had its fill of play this day."

"Fall back to the ledge," answered Halsedric. His sight did not stray long on his friend, his gaze snapping back quickly to the doorway once more. Snarls and screeches issued forth from the darkened space beyond, the sounds reverberating and bouncing along the stone. But only sounds issued forth. What haunted Halsedric stayed sheltered in the black of the tomb, just as he surmised.

Halsedric took one step backwards, then another, a rock pointing up and catching the heel of his sole. The errant stone made a sharp sound as it cracked against the granite walls of that natural void. Still, nothing came through that broken doorway, the evil within content to stay within the sheltering embrace of the shadows. With each step, the light of the outside world increased as the darkness gave way. He knew at once his instincts were correct. The dark was their only dwelling place, as befitting creatures of their foul make.

By now, Herodiani had come up from the stair, having briefly scouted the land from a suitable perch. As Halsedric took his last step out onto that ledge, he felt the hand of the Wodeman press against his back.

"Woah there," Tulvgir said. "Lest a pair of wings hide beneath that hauberk of yours. 'Tis a steep drop."

For a time, Halsedric stood there, tense, his eyes fixed upon that darkened doorway. Still, nothing ventured even into the shadows that gathered at the far end of the fissure. At least nothing he could see. Slowly he let the tip of his sword fall.

"What is your command?" Herodiani said, returning her sword to its scabbard.

Halsedric was slow to answer. "Our task here is complete, but I fear the peril is not." He pulled back his cloak, his face twisting as pain shot up from the wound on his arm. A soft click followed as the metal of his hilt made contact with the brass of the sheath. He held out his arm and inspected the wound. Blood soaked his sleeve as he pulled away pieces of torn cloth to inspect the damage done.

Herodiani stepped around him and leaned in to see for herself. Her eyes grew wide as she witnessed the torn flesh of his forearm. "We should bind that, and quick."

Flexing the fingers of his left hand, Halsedric turned his hand and wrist, inspecting the wound with a detached interest. His eyes narrowed as the pain made its presence known.

"No time," he replied, letting his arm fall.

"The Wodeman also has a wound—"

"Bah!" laughed Tulvgir. "None worse than a scratch."

"We need to be away from here," said Halsedric, his wounded arm swaying slightly as his attentions were drawn to the entrance of the tomb. He paused for a moment in thought. "I do not think our foe is yet done with us. We need to put as much distance as we can from this tomb ere night falls. For I fear his hounds will be loosed come the eventide."

Turing swiftly, his eyes went to the winding, treacherous stair. "We run when we find level ground."

Descending the stair was more difficult than ascending, save for Herodiani. Wounds made each handhold and footfall a lesson in agony that both Halsedric and Tulvgir bore well. Still, teeth ground together and a cry or two were stifled as a limb twisted or a wrong muscle flexed. The last stair was greeted with a certain amount of relish, though Tulvgir limped for the first few steps on solid ground.

Taking a moment to adjust their packs, Herodiani secured the blanket that held the bones with one hand, carrying her bow in the other. Their trail wound through the mounds, but stopped when they came to the figure in black that Herodiani felled.

Pulling a dagger from his belt, Halsedric knelt at the head of the mysterious figure. Clad foot to toe in black, stray feathers had detached from the cloak, some of them rolling over the stones that lay beneath as they were pushed by the breeze. The shaft of Herodiani's second arrow stuck up from its chest and moved up and down slightly, showing that life still remained beneath the sable garb. Pale flesh lay beneath the hood that still obscured the face of this strange sorcerer, and a sickening gurgling noise issued with each breath. Using the tip of his dagger, he pulled back some of the hood, revealing more. Daring his fingers, he went about exposing the face, as much as the arrow in its head would allow.

Beneath the hood lay a strange sight. It was the face of a man, though only with a passing glance. Dark hair was mingled with feathers, like that of the raven that called after them at their arrival. His skin was pale now as death drew near, dark blood having covered his lips and chin. He had a long nose bent down in a similar fashion to a crooked beak, from which more blood issued from the nostrils. The eyes, however, were an unexpected sight to behold. A solid, sickly yellow, a pupil split each one like the eyes of a cat. Open wide, they looked frozen, having no reaction to Halsedric as he pulled away more of the hood.

All of them looked on in a sickened sort of wonder, Herodiani being the only one to speak in that moment. "Is this the one we seek?"

"No," replied Halsedric. He let go of the hood and stood up, still looking down at the fallen man. Returning the dagger to his belt he added, "An acolyte, I think."

"A priest of the cult?" said Tulvgir taking the time to look around them.

"Perhaps," answered Halsedric. Pointing up at the ledge at the top of the stair, he added, "I think the foe we seek is there, in the darkness. And when night falls, he will come out from his hole and confront us."

He pivoted swiftly, looking at each of his two companions. To Tulvgir, however, he paid special attention. "Bind your wound here," he said to the Wodeman.

Thumping the head of his mace on the rock-strewn ground with a crunch, Tulvgir replied, "Bah! I've borne worse in my time." He spit on the ground in his defiance.

Halsedric smiled. "Your choice. Now, we must run."

CHAPTER 14

"Well, I must say, you were the quickest to come a-runnin' back here like flushed rabbits," the guide shouted with a cackle. Sitting on a folding stool near a low fire, he looked quite comfortable as he puffed on his short-stemmed pipe. The horses milled about behind him, two of them breaking away from the others, greeting the trio as they ran in from the forest beyond. Tulvgir fell to the ground heaving, a dark stain having covered the thigh of his trousers, evidence of how much blood had been lost.

The Wodeman rolled over on his back, stopped only by the pack he bore beneath his cloak. His hand reached out to grab at his wounded leg.

Leaves and dead pine needles crunched beneath the weight as Halsedric collapsed to his knees. The bones they gathered at the tomb made a muffled clacking sound as they fell from his hand. Breathing hard, he pulled at the hem of his cloak, using it to wipe the sweat from his brow.

Herodiani also fell forward, dropping her bow, her hands on her thighs as she doubled forward. While winded herself, she was the only one of the three not given over to total exhaustion, despite having to help Tulvgir on the last two miles of their dash. Two of the silvery-white mounts came to greet her as if she was a long-lost friend. Their tails waved and they nickered happily as they approached the Elanni maiden.

Using the stem of his pipe to point at the white horses, Drahm remarked, "Useful beasts they are, your mounts. Keepin' mine like shepherds an' their flocks. Where'd you get them?"

Through labored breaths, Halsedric called out, "Herodiani, heat a blade and tend to Tulvgir."

"Found a bit o' trouble, did you?" mocked Drahm, the tip of his pipe returning to his lips.

With a hard stare at the guide, Halsedric stood. He wiped his face with his cloak once more and made his way to the fire. "We need to break camp now."

"Do you now?" Drahm said with a puff on his pipe. "Tend your wounds, and we be off in the mornin'."

Halsedric replied tersely, "If we stay here, there will be no 'morrow."

"Found some treasure, did you?" Drahm replied, his head nodding at the crude pouch that lay on the ground. "Worth the trouble?"

"Those?" Halsedric said, turning back slightly. "Those are bones. Did you not hear me?"

"Ain't nev'r had no problems here," Drahm said, comfortable puffing on his pipe.

His eyes narrowing, Halsedric's eyes burned with anger. "Break camp or we leave here without you. Rather I risk the wilderness alone than what will descend upon us come eventide."

"And what might that be?"

Halsedric explained the events of only an hour or so before. As he spoke, Drahm's face, once mocking and defiant, fell into shock and concern. Head down, the guide plucked the pipe from his lips.

"We found two dozen, perhaps three," continued Halsedric. "And come night they will seek us out, of that I can assure you. Now, you can sit there and make jest at our misfortune, or you can break camp and follow." He shuffled about, facing back from whence they came. For a moment or two he stood there, his breath still labored from the run. In a low tone he said, "But, this I know. They are coming."

Once more, he faced the guide. "Our only hope now is distance. Put as much land between them and us. So, sit here, if you will, and doubt. Come moonrise, we shall see if you still mock."

Drahm merely sat there, head down, pipe in his hand. As Herodiani laid her dagger onto the hot coals, he stood up with a shot, turned his head and spat.

"Curse you an' all your kin," he grumbled. "Bringin' trouble in my camp. Bind your wounds an' let's be off then, revenant."

After cauterizing the wound on the thigh of the Wodeman and binding the bite on his arm with bandages, it took less than an hour to break camp and depart. This time, however, the caution that marked their arrival was thrown to the wind. They needed distance, and distance demanded speed.

The travel was not quick. There were no roads to take them there, leaving none for them on the return. Instead, it was game trails and open spaces where thick forests receded. Even through marshes they moved with haste, with always an eye on the sky and an anxious awareness of where the sun was above them. The horses were pushed hard. The silvery-white beasts Halsedric and his companions rode bore the burden well, seeming to never tire and always at risk of outpacing the beasts of their guide, much to his consternation.

Tulvgir bore the ordeal through gritted teeth. Despite the wound being closed and a mash of herbs to help it heal, the pain of it was worse than before. Each bump and turn was followed by a grumble, though when any of the others looked back in response, he showed no sign of his discomfort or discontent. Halsedric found this amusing, though he did his best to hide his true feelings. He knew Tulvgir had suffered worse.

It was a couple of hours before dusk when they finally stopped, finding a patch of land that jutted out onto a small lake. Here they unburdened their horses and set about clearing an open space and creating whatever defenses they could before the setting of the sun. With axe and sword, they quickly hewed young trees. They cleared ground around them with horse and rope, uprooting what could not be easily felled. Quickly, Drahm started a small camp fire while the others gathered what they could from the forest. Long dead branches, rotted sections of wood, dried leaves and needles, and clumps of pitch were piled and layered together along an arc from one end of the peninsula to the other, leaving a causeway in the middle for ingress and egress. As the last rays of light started to vanish below the western hills, what remained of their efforts was a crude picket of sorts protecting the small headland where they made their camp. Where the picket ended, mud and water shielded their flanks.

Cutting points into some of the saplings, they charred the tips in the flames to make crude spears. As the others labored, Halsedric gathered the horses of the Elanni outside of the fortification and spoke to them in a soft and foreign tongue. Drahm watched, perplexed as one of the Lenogala nodded as if acknowledging a command. The horses turned en masse, shepherding the other horses into the forest beyond.

The guide dropped his work and called out to Halsedric, "Aye! What madness is this?" His face turned red beneath the streaks of ash that covered his cheeks and nose as his voice bristled. Storming to the gap in the picket, axe in hand, he was met by Halsedric.

"What you think you a-doin'? Sendin' my beasts off into the woods?"

Hands up in an effort to calm the old guide, Halsedric replied in a cool tone, "Peace, friend. There is not enough room for both the horses and us."

Thrusting out the head of his axe as he spoke, Drahm snarled, "Fool! Don'tcha know there be wolves in these hills?"

"What follows comes for us, not for the beasts," answered Halsedric. "Your mounts will be well protected, far away from here." Pointing at the space behind him, he added, "There is not enough room for the horses and us in a fight. The last thing we need is for one of your beasts to spook in the midst of battle."

Drahm's eyes bulged and his mouth hung open with a huff. "I paid good coin for them beasts!" He turned excitedly and his eyes found Herodiani. She knelt nearby, gathering her arrows into her quiver. "Send her with `em, then," he added using his axe to point to the Elanni maiden.

"Herodiani?" answered Halsedric. "She will be up on a perch, keeping watch from above. Her bow is worth more than your horses, lest you place so little value on your own life."

For a moment, Drahm stood there staring but his anger was quickly cooled by his reason. "Bah," he exclaimed as he returned back to his work. "No gold was worth this folly," he barked angrily as a parting remark.

Halsedric stepped through the gap and watched the old guide walk away, every sound coming out of Drahm's mouth a curse of one sort or another. Halsedric's head turned to Herodiani.

With a nod, she collected her arrows and slung the quiver around her shoulder before making for the causeway.

CHAPTER 15

With a grunt, Drahm thrust the end of the make-shift torch into the hard ground of their camp. He had made six in all fashioned from split branches. Into these was set a pinecone with every gap and crevice filled with melted pitch. These they made ready to set fire to the pickets when the appointed time came.

From the gear they piled nearby, he took out his folding stool with a leather seat. Axe in hand, he made his way over to where Halsedric stood by the gap. As Halsedric drew his sword from its sheath, Drahm laid down his axe and unfolded his stool. Collapsing into his seat, he huffed as he used the back of his hand to wipe the sweat from his brow.

Thrusting the tip of his blade into the ground, Halsedric slunk down, taking a place next to the barricade a few paces away. Finally done with a long day's work, he leaned against a barrier of bound saplings that protected the central causeway. Staves fashioning into crude spears stuck out like massive quills, lashed to a triangular base using pine roots as cordage. Hardened by fire, the tips of the spears were blackened. The structure creaked in response to Halsedric's weight.

"Ho, there," Drahm warned. "Not too much of you on there. I don't need you undoin' all my work."

Staked into place at the bottom, it was secure enough to defend what might come at it from the front. However, it was no grand spectacle of engineering in the least. It was as good as the available material.

Halsedric looked up at the barrier and pulled away, being wary to undo all the effort that made it.

For a time, the pair sat in silence, Drahm looking around at all they had accomplished. "We'll need a man at both ends when they come." He paused for a moment, adding under his breath, "If'n they come."

Halsedric spread out on the ground, a padding of debris and wood chips being his only blanket that night. "If they do not come, all we have lost is time and sweat."

"If'n they do? How many?"

"How far do you think we journeyed this day?"

Drahm looked at his hands introspectively. His fingers and his palms were covered with dirt, sticky pitch, and ash. "Four leagues. Mayhaps less, if'n I recollect true."

Head falling, Halsedric pondered. "They do not favor the light, that is assured. From the tomb to the camp to here? A long way here and back ere the sun rises once more."

"An' if'n all this for naught?"

Halsedric inhaled deeply and let it out with a rush. "I would rather look a fool than be a fool, leaving us undefended."

"Aye," Drahm said with a nod.

"If you had two of the Lenogala as your mounts, we could ride through night into day. Alas, this was not so."

"If'n my beasts—" Drahm said, sitting up straight. Halsedric was quick to answer.

"Your beasts are far safer with ours than they will be here, that I assure you."

Grumbling, Drahm leaned forward again. For a time, the pair was silent, giving Drahm the opportunity to inspect Halsedric. His attention went to the surcoat. "What does it say?"

"What?"

"The runes."

Halsedric looked down, inspecting the golden lettering on his stained and dingy surcoat. "Oh, these? I do not know."

"Why wear 'em?"

"They were given to me by the prophet after I was returned from death. Divine Script, I think."

At that moment, Halsedric lifted himself up and turned himself around on the ground. He held out his wounded arm, trying to catch the dim firelight. Unknotting the bandage, he unwrapped the wound partly, leaned in, and inspected the damage. Flexing his fingers repeatedly, he monitored the wound. Using a little spittle and his thumb to clear the dried blood revealed the extent of the wound and just how much had been restored. There was no bleeding now, despite bandages soaked near black. Bright pink replaced raw maroon-tinged flesh in places where the fangs of the fiend that bit him tore away muscle and skin. A grievous wound for some. To Halsedric, a painful annoyance.

"This may take a day or two yet to heal."

Drahm leaned in and got a look for himself. "By the gods," he muttered, perplexed at the sight.

"Still, you do not believe?"

"You ask much 'o believin'" answered Drahm. "A curious one you are." After a quick silence as Halsedric started to wrap the wound once more, he asked, "What saw you up in that tomb?"

"It wasn't what I saw, but what I felt."

"Aye?"

Halsedric stopped his work, thinking for a second. "Something remembered from my first mission, long ago. When I slew the prophetess." With that, Halsedric fell silent, appearing to inspect his wound. His gaze, however, seemed far away from the moment.

"Aye?" Drahm prompted, intrigued.

Halsedric's head twitched slightly as his wounded arm fell. It was as if he was trying to shake some long-forgotten facts loose deep within his memory. "Could be nothing."

"Mayhaps," Drahm replied. He was beginning to lose interest. His attention went to his hands, rubbing them together in the vain attempt to clean them off.

"I remember, deep in that cave." Halsedric's voice was whispery at first, growing with intensity as each image of that fateful moment turned clear and distinct in his recollection. "I had slain her last protector. I was wounded far worse than now," he said.

He began to wrap the wound again, continuing his tale. His voice turned low and his words turned ominous. "She did little to defend herself, letting her stone daggers fall to the ground. Daggers she had once used to cut out the hearts of men, sacrificing them to her new gods."

Drahm became enthralled with the tale. Arms on his knees, he leaned forward, "An' what then? A dagger hidin' in the boot?"

With a shake of his head, Halsedric answered, "No. That was not her way."

"What then?"

"She tried to seduce me," Halsedric answered, looking up. "Soft words, not steel. That was her way. She left the killing to others. Followers. Fanatics."

He stopped for a moment, taking time to pull the last ends of the bandage taut on his arm and knotting the bandage. One end in his teeth, the other in his fingers, he pulled, securing the cloth on his arm, testing how well it held afterwards. "She even swayed a friend of mine to her cause."

"An' then?"

As he looked up once more to the guide, Halsedric's pale eyes turned as chilled and final as a marble sepulcher. "I slew them. All."

"Your friend? An' an unarmed maid?"

"Yes," Halsedric answered with a slow nod.

"Cold," replied Drahm with a passionless stare.

"Perhaps," Halsedric answered. "It was my mission."

"For this God of yours?" Drahm's words dripped derision.

Quick to answer, Halsedric's words were firm. "You did not witness the bodies hanging from trees. Nor did you see the altars stained with the blood of those sacrificed in her name or in the reverence to her gods. In some places, only a few remained hidden in cellars, rude burrows dug out beneath homes. Starving. Near death. I have seen too much to hold regret for the deeds I was tasked to do."

As a silence fell over the two, Halsdric's head fell as the memories returned, even clearer now. "As she lay dying, something cried in the darkness. Something deep in the dark, just outside of my senses or understanding. Old. Reveling in the shadows, wearing them as a cloak. Filled with such hatred and malevolence, I could scarce breathe."

"An' that you found in the tomb, aye?"

Once more, another long pause as he considered his next word. "No. Not as strong, yet reeking of the same stench of evil."

Shifting on the ground a bit, he continued, his words having less gravity than before. "I have contested with much evil since that day, each form of it having its own unique reek. None, however, like what I sensed in that cave—until now."

His gaze seeking that of Drahm, he said, "You spoke of ghosts when we first met, yes?"

"Aye."

"This was such a ghost, lingering somewhere in a corner of deep shadow. Pulled from death, lingering in the twilight gap between life and unlife. Held there by a will few in this world possess. A torn shred from a larger cloth, lesser in stature but whose color is just as sickening and vile. Hidden away, waiting, reconstituting its former self. That was my mission. That is what I found. And now that I have revealed it, I sense that it will come for us all. For we hold its secret."

"An' that secret be?" said Drahm.

"That it lives once more," replied Halsedric. "That it has been growing a new host of its own with each and every fool lured to that hole. Fools seeking a treasure that never was."

Drahm thought on this for a moment as the crackling of the campfire filled the silence that lingered beneath them. Somewhere in the distance, Tulvgir hummed a song he knew, contenting himself in the light offered up by the flames.

"You say—"

"It was all a ruse," interrupted Halsedric. Words whispered into the ears of the avaricious seeking quick riches. Greedy hearts who found their way to you."

It didn't take a keen sense of direction to know where the conversation was going, Drahm connecting the dots as the warrior spoke. Every single one the victims Halsedric mentioned, Drahm had led them to their doom, unwittingly or no. Sitting straight up, Drahm's eyes went as wide as saucers. "You don't mean—"

"Calm your fears," answered Halsedric, his words dismissing Drahm's fears.

"I warned each an' every one of `em," protested the guide.

"As you warned me." Halsedric raised his hand. "Repeatedly. Calm yourself. If I suspected as such, I would have slain you long before now. I certainly would not have taken the time and trouble to tell you all of this."

It took a moment before Drahm began to relax. Rubbing the scar along his jaw, reviving the bad memory of the moment the wound was visited upon him. His bulging eyes lessened. Once more he leaned forward. "What next, aye?"

"We wait. I will pray for our victory."

Drahm inhaled deeply and looked to his filthy hands once more.

They passed the hours that followed eating a meal they all hoped would not be their last. Drahm had another thick slice of his Trapper's Cake, Halsedric taking a couple of handfuls of parched corn, normally reserved for cakes, and eating it straight from the pouch. While Herodiani kept watch hidden in the boughs of a tree, Tulvgir chewed on a piece of dried beef near the fire. The moon rose high in the sky as they fed the campfire, the mood turning grim and quiet among the four defenders.

As the night went on, a shrill whistle broke the tense silence. Drahm looked up from his stool anxiously as Halsedric lifted from his place on the ground by the barricade.

Halsedric's sword hummed, the shining steel turning a pale red. The glow of it showed along the spine, as if heated from within. The sight of it came as such a surprise that it knocked Drahm from his chair in shock.

Adrenaline seeping into his veins, the old man rolled over, grabbed his axe, and stood clumsily as Halsedric scrambled to his feet.

"Light the torches. To your places," Halsedric shouted.

At once, there was a flurry of activity. Halsedric pulled his sword from the ground, the glow of his blade growing as evil drew ever nearer. Drahm and Tulvgir raced to the torches, grabbing three apiece. Each thrust one into the campfire to set it alight before they departed to their places along the line. Tulvgir moving with purposeful steps to the right, Drahm to the left, their torches held high.

With their torches spitting and popping, the guide and the Wodeman set the tinder of their crude pickets alight. A slow process at first, the tinder casually caught the flame. As their torches started to fail, they lit another, continuing their task until each reached the water's edge. There they waited, weapons held at the ready.

Halsedric moved less excitedly. His eyes peered out from the gaps in the barricade, spying the darkness past the wall. His mind went briefly to Herodiani in her perch in the trees. Wondering if she was safe, he prayed silently for her protection. The color of his blade continued to grow and change as time ticked by. The flames along the wall grew slowly, and he eyed them nervously, wondering if the blazing barrier he imagined in his head was a fool's errand. Pockets of pitch and needles sizzled and popped as flames spontaneously ejected up and out along the wall. Still his blade grew redder, the center of the glow now a cherry red.

The cracking of twigs and the rustle of grass blended with the sound of burning wood and tinder. Smoke billowed upward as the fire spread, now engorged by pieces of fatwood and dry, dead limbs. As it rose, a cloud gathered, acrid and hazy in the still air. Amidst the fog, firelight extended its dominion over the dark, diffused and softened. As if spurred by the consuming fire, Halsedric's sword burst into flames, letting him know that evil was near. As he looked again past the barricade, peering past the ribbons that rose from the defensive pyre, his searching eyes spied pale forms moving in the murk. He counted them, quietly at first, hoping to glean the numbers of the foe. Two, four, seven, maybe more just inside the fringe of darkness that cloaked them. They moved as animals. Some paced partially upright, others with a hunched gait, moving on all fours.

Then he felt it. Dim and distant at first, but unmistakable. The same sensation he felt in the dark of the tomb made its presence known, the hair rising on the back of his head and a sickness welling in his gut. From between the gaps of the barricade, he scanned the gloom, finding nothing but darkness and shifting forms barely cloaked by the night.

It had been a long time since Halsedric felt fear. The last time being when that axe fell down upon him, taking his life those many years long past. A memory tucked away in the furthest recesses of his mind, recalled from time to time so as not to forget the sensation of terror. The fear now was powerful and sharp, not unlike the thrust of a spear.

An unmistakable hiss rose from the wilderness beyond, punctuated by foul screeching. More movement as the flames grew along the makeshift wooden wall. Once-hazy forms in the black now sharpened in clarity, the details of their appearance becoming distinct. The sickening hue of their milky white flesh told Halsedric all he needed to know. These devils were the same he found deep in that tomb. The very same ones who chased him to the doorway. Now, like the hounds of some baleful master they had hunted and pursued those who dared violate the accursed sanctity of that black tomb.

Halsedric watched intently as the fiends moved along the perimeter of their defenses like ravenous rabid wolves facing an obstacle they could not fathom or overcome. Scurrying this way and that, their movements mimicked pack hunters, seeking a weakness in their defenses. Halsedric counted again – three, eight, ten. Ten of them, he was sure now. He called out their number to the others, his hand gripping tight the hilt of his blade, his body tensing, ready for a fight.

With screeches and howls, the pale monstrosities attacked, their numbers scattering along the length of the wall. Several made for the ends while a few headed straight for the barricade where Halsedric stood guard.

A form leapt into the air attempting to vault over the spikes, a move both mindless and bold. The timber creaked and cracked when the attempt failed, the creature impaling itself on one of the sapling spears. It twitched and flailed in its death throes, letting out a strangled cry as the barricade groaned in reply. Hands grabbed at the timbers, quickly dashed away by the point of Halsedric's sword. One unlucky minion slammed its head against the wooden grid, its sepia eyes closed, and those horrible fangs chewing at the green wood and cordage. This warranted a fatal wound as Halsedric thrust his sword in the gaps. Pierced deep in its flesh and bone, the monster fell where it stood, slipping off the tip of the burning blade. Undaunted, new hands assaulted the structure, attempting to tear away the crude barrier standing in their way.

Cinders erupted from the burning wall as it shook, followed by the harrowing screams of the attackers on the other side. He didn't need to look to know what was happening. Barred by the spikes and timbers, some of the pale fiends attempted to dismantle the flaming structure, creating a breach. Heat and licking tongues of fire greeted them, greedily consuming their once living flesh. Even as talons and fangs tore at the spikes, the wall shuttered and shook. With each screech and scream, ash and hot sparks lifted into the air.

A portion of the wall fell, a dip forming along the high ridge. Soon after, two bald bloated heads poked up at the newly formed gap, revealing activity amidst the flames. Howling and baying their horrible cries, they contested with the fire that tore at them with ember and flame. A hiss came from beyond, an arrow cutting the air, hitting one of the forms somewhere in the midst of its back. Herodiani, from her perch on high, found her mark, the missile flying true.

While not a fatal blow, it was enough for the attacker to pause and turn, shifting its weight on an unstable ramp. Its taloned hand slipped through a gap, becoming stuck as a burning branched collapsed atop it. As hard as it was to imagine the sounds from such a creature being any worse than they were, a horrifying sound came from the trapped and burning thing as the fire had its fill.

The other leaped past the dip in the wall, the flames doing their best to keep it at bay. As it tumbled down the other side, Halsedric was there, both hands on the hilt of his sword, the many-colored flames rising from the blade. His stroke was swift and sure, decapitating the creature as it recovered, leaving the detached portion of its head bouncing along the ground. Even as the headless form slumped, his foot came around, hitting it square, pushing the remains into the fire, where it started to burn, limbs twitching.

More dread fingers laid hands to the timbers that held the makeshift spears firm at the gap. Cordage creaked, the fibers fraying as Halsedric thrust his sword through the gaps. With a shout of righteous anger, the tip of his weapon found cold pale flesh. A rending shriek followed the stab. The tip of another talon cut the flesh of his arm, causing him to grimace in pain as he withdrew. Undaunted, he thrust his sword in again and again, randomly and in rapid succession giving whatever lay beyond cause for pause. Smoke penetrated his nostrils as sulfurous fumes reached deeply into his lungs. His eyes watered as he coughed. He had hoped for a breeze to carry away the dense screen that formed. None ever came.

As the assault at the causeway lessened, Halsedric heard a hard, shrill cry. "Breech!"

"Drahm," he muttered to himself. The cry came from Drahm.

CHAPTER 16

When Halsedric found Drahm, he had a dagger in one hand and a burning torch of pitch in the other. Three of the invaders were closing in on him. Barely scrambling to his feet in time, the guide waved the torch wildly with a loud cracked shout. The dagger lunged wildly, threatening, giving the creatures a moment of pause to consider their actions. Yet, their fear of fire was enough to hold them at bay, though only momentarily.

Drahm's right arm was bleeding at the shoulder, the nails of one of the creatures rent through leather and flesh in a swipe. The old man, however, was not helpless in any way. Two of the creatures lay dead nearby, one with his axe embedded deep in his skull. Body lying face down, the attacker had fallen where water met the land. Another lay nearby, two white-fletched arrows sticking up from its lifeless form. One of the darts had found a home in its back, another in the back of its head.

Halsedric crashed into the creature threatening Drahm's left flank, plowing into it with his shoulder. With a thump, the creature flew backwards into the water with a screech. Water splashed as the creature flailed. The roar of Halsedric's sword filled the air, the sound of it mingling with the snap and crackle of the burning wall.

When the blade fell, it hit the second attacker square across the back, nearly cleaving the thing in two.

Drahm looked on in stunned amazement as Halsedric went after the two other fiends, kicking one into the flaming wall. As the other recovered its stance, it thrust itself at the warrior, its right talon swiping at him wildly. As the arm came back for a second pass, Halsedric caught it by the wrist, pulling the monster to his awaiting sword, impaling it on his blade. With a throaty grunt, he lifted his blade upwards, slicing flesh and bone as if it were nothing more than sackcloth. The blade exited through the dying beast's right shoulder, followed by a dark spray.

He let go of the wrist of the dying thing and let it fall as he attended to the third, smoke rising from the flames. The crude loincloth it wore about its waist was alight, and its pale flesh smoldered.

Lifting his blade high in the air, Halsedric cleaved the creature square across its bloated crown. The cut was severe, splitting the head in two, the stroke ending somewhere in its upper chest. With a grunt, he pulled the blade free, letting the body crumple where it once stood.

Halsedric paused, breathing hard, black viscera and blood spotting his clothes and face. As he turned to face Drahm, he witnessed the old man staring at him, eyes wide, face fallen, the light of the fire placing shadows on the creases in his skin.

All Drahm could offer was a stunned whisper. "By the gods."

Hearing the words, Halsedric frowned as he grumbled his displeasure. Now, in the thick of battle, was not the time to correct the old guide in his beliefs.

Head tilted to one side, Halsedric noted Drahm's wound once more. "Can you fight?"

"Aye?" The stupor and bewilderment had not yet faded from Drahm, the old man speechless at the speed and ferocity of Halsedric's attack. After a moment, he turned his head and moved his arm slightly, wincing as he did. "Aye. I can fight."

As the flames of his blade noisily burned away the corrupted flesh and blood that stained them, Halsedric commanded, "Grab your axe then and hold the line."

A shrill warbling whistle from beyond the wall followed, Halsedric's ears receiving it woefully. Concern flooded his face as his eyes looked past the old man to the causeway.

"The center has been breeched," he said as he moved swiftly to the barricade.

Forms came out of the smoke to greet him, Halsedric closing on them halfway. The first lunged at him, a talon slashing wildly and missing. Pulling his blade back, being too close, he countered with the back of the hand to the creature's maw. The blow landed with a crunch, knocking the fiend away, stunning it momentarily.

A second came out of the acrid mist, followed close by a third. Vaulting into the air, it came at Halsedric with talons out.

Stepping aside, Halsedric turned as the creature tumbled to the ground, rolling over and exposing its abdomen. Here, he thrust his blade, the holy steel piercing the creature through, cutting deep into the earth, pinning it in place.

Even as he did, the claws of the other raked at Halsedric's back, finding their mark. He cried out as leather and cloth gave way, two sharp tips cutting flesh like the tips of daggers. The pain ran through him like a sudden fire, stealing away his breath. For a moment, he hesitated. The monstrosity fell to the side, its attack leaving it off-balance.

Drawing a dagger from his belt, Halsedric swerved away from a second swipe, then a third, before grappling with the fiend. The action of the foe was as quick as those of a viper, but Halsedric was quicker. Pinning one arm beneath his right knee, and holding another with his left arm, he switched his grip on his dagger. As his opponent's head lurched forward to sink its fangs into the flesh of his thigh, Halsedric came down with the blade of his knife, slamming it deeply into the temple of its bloated head with a harrowing crunch. Limbs shuddered, and the throat of the pale fiend gave a stuttering warble for a moment before its body weakened and went limp.

Leaving the dagger in the beast, Halsedric rolled off the dying foe. Standing unsteady at first, he went to the monster he pinned to the ground. The thing still lived, its clawed hands vainly grasped at the blade and the hilt trying to pull it free. It was all to no avail. The flames of the holy steel burned it each time its flesh made contact with the steel. Each attempt was followed by screeches and cries as its milky gray flesh seared and burned, the weapon rejecting the unclean hands that dared to touch it.

Wounded and hurting, Halsedric moved slower now. From the campfire, he pulled a burning branch, grasping it by a length untouched by fire. Staggering over to the trapped thing, he took the branch with both hands and laid two devastating blows to its skull. Charcoal and embers flew up with each hammer blow, the second snapping the branch in half along the burnt end. Lazily tossing the branch aside, his hand reclaimed his holy brand, pulling out from flesh and earth as he turned towards the causeway. His back still burning from deep lacerations, Halsedric pushed into the enveloping smoke, coughing as he did. Sweat rolled down his brow, the droplets stinging his eyes. He found the barricade, portions of it broken, and pushed away. Along with a missing section of the wall at the causeway, a gap had been made, allowing attackers to file in. Yet, as he took his place there, awaiting the onrush of others, none came.

He coughed once more. Thick choking smoke surrounded him, forcing a withdrawal. The fire on the wall burned hot and wild now. Darkness pushed away with the force of its untamed light. Eyes stinging and squinting, he held his blade at the ready. Still, nothing came.

"Tulvgir? Report." His voice rose high and hard, contesting with the roar of the burning wall. When the Wodeman did not answer, he shouted the name again.

"Four slain," came Tulvgir's reply. "Quiet here."

"Drahm?"

"Clear," answered Drahm, his voice weak and thin.

Seconds passed, then he heard Herodiani's whistle. A long, high tone that turned low before the end. A sure signal that all was clear from her perch.

Halsedric stepped back again, quiet but still tense and anxious. He searched his feelings, felt the tingle still in his gut. Raising his blade upright, his eyes scanned the weapon with confused wonder. The blade was still hot, and the colored flames danced along its length. Evil was still at hand, no doubt waiting just beyond the flames and the smoke.

For many moments he wondered, his eyes looking at the holy runes that ran the length of the spine, barely visible beneath the cherry red glow of the steel. It was still out there, whatever it may be. He remembered dots of red light against the black of the tomb's interior, its pale creations a barrier between the holy warrior and whatever lay in the shadows. A dark shade in the black pit of that tomb. Ghosts, as Drahm noted in that seedy tavern.

"Hold your ground," Halsedric called out to the others, his voice strained by the command. Thrusting the tip of his blade into the ground, he plunged once more into the smoke. The breeze picked up as the stinging smell of the obscuring smog whirled around him. Laying hands on the barricade they worked so hard to construct, he pulled at the frame of it. The flesh of his back burned as his muscles flexed and tensed, cordage snapping, green wood shearing and twisting, finally giving way at the third pull. What remained scraped dirt and stone as it shuddered, widening the opening big enough for him to slip through without being singed by the flames.

Returning to his sword, he pulled it from the dirt and slipped though the gap. He could feel the intensity of the raging blaze at his back. It was a welcome feeling to be free of the heat and smoke as he stepped out into the open land beyond.

Before him lay tramped grasses and ferns among the holes where the roots of trees once clung to the ground. Halsedric moved warily as another sensation reached out to him, something foreign and eerily familiar, long forgotten in a past life. A life where death and its long sleep faced a man in the heat of battle. A familiar sort of fear, it was before him, wrapping itself around him, like a substitute of the smoke from whence he came. He knew its smell, but no longer fell weak to its grip.

Looking around, his blade still burning bright in the presence of the unholy, he wondered from whence this ill tide came. Raising his sword high, he called out to the night and the darkened wilderness beyond.

"I am the wielder of the Holy Flame. He that has died, and raised again. Warrior of the God of the West, and the lands of the hallowed therein. I command you, come forth, dark spirit. Show yourself, evil shade, and make yourself known."

His words echoed through the trees, the burning and cracking of the raging fire behind him reclaiming the quiet as the sound of his voice died away. Long moments passed as he waited in the night, his back burning, his eyes still stinging, straining to see beyond the shadows of the night.

Before him, many paces in the distance, two pin-pricks showed themselves against the dark, like cinders ejected from the fire behind him. Surrounding them, a form appeared like smoke and shadow. Black against black, it appeared as a hole in the deep of the night. Lingering there, suspended just above the ground, wisps of its incorporeal form danced and twisted along the fringe like trails of hazy gloom, vaguely human.

"Proclaim yourself, I command you," shouted Halsedric, his voice booming with every word.

In the silence that followed, a single word was said in response, like the hiss of a viper, and the rumbling growls of the mountain wurms of the east. "Asteroth," it said.

"Come forth and lay steel to mine, and let us be done with this, foul creature," Halsedric answered, taking his sword in both hands, feet apart, preparing for a fight.

The shade did nothing, simply hanging there in the air for a moment, unmoving, unfazed.

"Come at me," Halsedric demanded.

Instead, the shade lurched forward, hazy limbs back, like a lion lunging towards a kill. With an ear-rending screech, it answered him with the only action it knew. There was a rumble and a pop, and the air around it filled with a stink. Trails and tendrils of blacked smoke hung in the air where the shade once stood, twisting in the newfound breeze that blew through the trees. Oily and sickening, they dispersed, then vanished, leaving only their stench and the darkness of the wilderness. In time, the roar of the burning wall was the only sound that re-mained in the night.

Halsedric relaxed as the flames from his sword dimmed and the sheen of his steel reclaimed the blade. The evil that troubled them was gone, leaving behind an unwholesome reek.

CHAPTER 17

Threads of smoke wafted into the camp as the sun's rays broke the mountaintops. The wall that protected them, rising like an inferno, was now mounds of coal, ash, and embers. Flames still rose, though their power was now greatly diminished. Charred remains of the dead lay littered along the length of it, the pallid flesh now withered and scorched. They had thrown the fallen attackers into the consuming fires, to ensure that what was dead remained thus. Little more than brittle threads of sinew clung to blackened bones. Misshapen skulls peered out from the coals, their maws fallen open, their sinister fangs rendered harmless. What was once corrupted was now cleansed from the land, purged from the world.

With a grunt, Halsedric's eyes slammed tight as Herodiani knotted the bandages that were wrapped around his chest and shoulders. Such pain only came with deep gashes, the rent remains of his surcoat a testament to that fact. Two deep gashes of red bled openly as the Elanni huntress started tending to them.

"These are the last of the bandages," said Herodiani, twisting two ends of the white gauze, completing the knot.

Halsedric's wounds were the last to be tended, by his own insistence. In addition to his leg, Tulvgir's left forearm was also slashed, though the marring was not as deep. He bore the pain of both wounds well as he tended to the cakes cooking on the coals of the campfire. The only hint of his condition was an evident limp and dark stains on the cloth that bound the cut on his leg. The Wodeman hummed a song, using a stick to flip the flat breads on the heat.

Drahm sat on his stool nearby, head in his hands, worn from the night's efforts, but otherwise showing little fatigue. His arm and shoulder bound as best as they could be, he insisted his nurse cut away the rent leather and cloth before tending the wound.

Ash staining his hand, Halsedric retrieved his surcoat. He shuffled through the layers, looking at the section that covered his back and noting the marks. Once pure white, the garment was filthy, stained with blood, gray ash, and dirt. Torn from one hem midway through the width of the garment, threads of golden trim stuck out like stray hairs. He sighed before letting it fall to the ground.

Herodiani, finished with her tasks, stood and saw Halsedric's despair. "It can be mended."

"This I know," Halsedric answered her in a tired voice. "And cleaned."

Fingers extended, Halsedric flipped his hands over and back again. In addition to being filthy, black soot had built up under his fingernails and layered around his cuticles. In fact, the whole gathering was filthy, save for Herodiani. She was spared the worst of the battle up there in her perch in the trees.

"What next?" the huntress asked of him as she knelt to pick up her quiver. Most of the spent arrows she recovered, though three were lost.

Head tilting up and back, Halsedric stared at her out of the corner of his eyes. Garbed in green, her long, flaxen hair was pulled back into a long braid and bound in a decorative knot behind her head. Blue eyes stared back at him, expectant.

"Call the horses, I think. And eat. See if we can douse what flames remain before we are gone."

Drahm seemed to revive at the mere mention of leaving. His head popped up from his hands and weary eyes focused on Halsedric. He cleared his throat before scratching his beard along the scar on his jaw. "Where to?"

Both Herodiani and Halsedric looked to Drahm with puzzlement. Halsedric spoke. "Take us to the nearest village, if you will. We will find our way to the coast from there."

His arms folding on his legs, Drahm leaned forward. His bottom lip thrust itself up and out, almost making it look as if he were pouting. Drahm, however, was not a man for sobbing and tears. His eyes shifted about as he pondered something deep.

"You do not seem much convinced of our plan," Herodiani spoke after putting the strap of her quiver over her shoulder.

"Oh, it's not that," Drahm replied, his eyes distant. Silence followed, his words lingering in the air as the other three waited patiently.

Even before Halsedric could ask, Drahm spoke again. "I was figurin' you might need a guide still. To the coast an' all."

Halsedric looked stunned, eyes blinking their utter disbelief. Herodiani echoed this sentiment, her actions slowed, and her eyes widening with a sort of mild confusion.

"What say you?" said Halsedric, totally befuddled.

"I know a sure path to th' coast, if'n you have th' coin."

Mouth trembling at first, not quite knowing what to say, Halsedric eventually spoke. "I for certain—"

"Well, there's Jethlo an' his kin a-waitin' for me. Him I'd like to miss."

"Yet—"

"After all, them bones you got must be 'o some import if'n you care so much to bring 'em along," Drahm broke in.

"Elenur," Herodiani spoke. The word came free and fluid from her lips, spoken in her native tongue.

"Wassthat?" answered Drahm.

"Elenur," said Halsedric, the name itself sounding flat on his tongue. "The mighty kingdom of the Elanni. Her home."

"Call it what you will," said Drahm, his left hand lifting as he spoke.

"King Loenoquai reigns there, one of the oldest of her kin," Halsedric answered, motioning to the huntress. "We must report our findings, for grave tidings we bear. He, too, will have understanding of the remains we carry. Whether they should be laid to rest, or returned to the Uttermost West."

His attention returning to Drahm, Halsedric stared blankly at the old guide. Shaking his head slightly as if unable to believe what he was hearing, he asked, "I assumed that after the trouble we put you through—"

"Aye," Drahm said with a somber nod. "Trouble you are. Not worth th' coin, neither."

"And yet?"

Reluctance halted his words, every sign of it showing on the old man's face. When he did answer, it came out haltingly at first. "A man sees things. Things he don't believe at first, if'n you know what I mean."

"Do you fear the return of the specter?"

"Aye," replied Drahm after a moment, his voice soft and low. "If'n you be right, an' those that know be mark'd. Might be such things come for me in the night. Aye?"

"Is that all?" asked Herodiani.

"No," Drahm said with a shake of his head. His voice sounded uncertain, even timid, for him. "I was a-thinkin', if'n you're willin' to tell me more about this God of yours. The one that gave you that burnin' sword an' all. Teach me to pray to Him, like you did. Have Him hear my words."

Herodiani leaned into Halsedric and spoke something in her native tongue. She was stilled when Halsedric raised his hand, bidding her stop.

"What's she a-sayin'?" Drahm asked, suspicious.

"Our path takes us to Elenur," replied Halsedric.

"Makes no diff'rnce to me."

"Mortal men are not welcome in the lands of the Ageless," Herodiani answered, the words rolling off her tongue, rich like honey.

Drahm's eyes fell. A long, noisy exhale followed. It was like a siren that spoke of his disappointment.

"However, exceptions have been made. In the past, if I am not mistaken." Halsedric's voice was hopeful, and his face pleased, if only slightly.

"Yes, this is true," Herodiani said with a nod, though her expression was dour in comparison to her comrade.

Drahm looked up suddenly, a spark kindling a fire in his gaze. "Aye?"

"But the road will not be without peril," said Halsedric.

Sitting up straight, hands on his knees, one brow lifted high as the guide said dubiously, "Worse than this? Aye?"

"Cathars and Yerch. You said so yourself. The road will be hard."

"These old bones ain't none too weary for anotha' adventure before I'm done. If'n you know what I mean. What be Elenur like?" said Drahm.

"Filled with wonder," answered Halsedric.

And so it was, before the noontime came and went, the party was gone from the battlefield. Headed south and west, they made their way to the shore of the Sorrowing Sea, in search of a ship to take them due south to the enchanted realm of Elenur.

Of what became of Drahm, little else is known. Whether his old eyes saw the wonders of those blessed lands, no mortal knows and none of the Ageless say. What is known, however, was that before he passed, he came into the worship of the Allfather, the eternal God of the West, and remained so until his days were done.

Halsedric, however, still had many more adventures before him.

9 780578 359298